THE INQUIRER

THE INQUIRER

JACLYN DAWN

NEWEST PRESS
EDMONTON, AB

Library and Archives Canada Cataloguing in Publication

Title: The inquirer / Jaclyn Dawn.
Names: Dawn, Jaclyn, 1984- author.
Series: Nunatak first fiction series ; no. 51.
Description: Series statement: Nunatak first fiction series ; 51
Identifiers: Canadiana (print) 20190072210 |
Canadiana (ebook) 20190072253 |
ISBN 9781988732671 (softcover) |
ISBN 9781988732688 (EPUB) |
ISBN 9781988732695 (Kindle) |
Classification: LCC PS8607.A95985 I57 2019 | DDC C813/.6—dc23

Editor for the Press: Leslie Vermeer
Cover and interior design: Kate Hargreaves
Back cover photo by Ethan Haddox via Unsplash
Author photo: Michelle Wurban, One Shot Photography

NeWest Press acknowledges the Canada Council for the Arts, the Alberta Foundation for the Arts, and the Edmonton Arts Council for support of our publishing program. We acknowledge the financial support of the Government of Canada through the Canada Book Fund for our publishing activities.

NeWest Press wishes to acknowledge that the land on which we operate is Treaty 6 territory and a traditional meeting ground and home for many Indigenous Peoples, including Cree, Saulteaux, Niitsitapi (Blackfoot), Métis, and Nakota Sioux.

NeWest Press
#201, 8540-109 Street
Edmonton, Alberta T6G 1E6
NeWest Press www.newestpress.com

No bison were harmed in the making of this book.
PRINTED AND BOUND IN CANADA

1 2 3 4 5 21 20 19

For every woman who has hidden behind a smile

PROLOGUE

KINGSLEY GROCERY WAS OF A DYING BREED IN ALBERTA, found only in small towns. An old building with mismatched shelving, faded linoleum, and chipped paint. It was too warm in the summer and too cold in the winter, which was hell on the perishables. It might be better described as a convenience store than a grocery store. The new Minimart off the highway next to the truck stop was better: newer, bigger, cheaper.

And yet everyone shopped at Kingsley Grocery at least a couple times a month. Most made excuses. They said they stopped for the convenience. Kingsley Grocery was, after all, sandwiched between the bank and the hardware store in the heart of town. They stopped for the home-baked goods. The owner's wife, Mrs. Wong, sold her rock-hard cookies and dry squares at the counter. They stopped for the quick checkout, although the three tills at the Minimart could hardly be described as busy. They also said they wanted to support small business owners in the community, even if that meant paying five dollars more for a carton of eggs, a gallon of milk, and a loaf of bread, all of which would spoil a week sooner than the same purchases made at the Minimart. Few admitted the real reason everyone chose Kingsley Grocery.

The newspaper rack stood at the end of the counter. On the bottom shelf was the *Edmonton Journal*, the middle the *Edmonton Sun*, and the top the *Kingsley Inquirer*. Alongside the papers was a locked box the size of a dinner roast with '*Kingsley Inquirer: Advertisment, Submision & Payment*' misspelt on the side. Even Mr. Wong claimed not to know who was behind the *Inquirer*, but Kingsley Grocery was the only store that sold it.

The *Inquirer* was the real reason people shopped at Kingsley Grocery.

KINGSLEY

INQUIRER

BEER BUTT CHICKEN RECIPE INSIDE!!!

TRULA DISCOVERS ROLAND'S ONLINE DATING ACCOUNT

- 13-YEAR MARRIAGE IN RUINS
- KIDS DEVASTATED
- 'LET ME EXPLAIN' ROLAND PLEADS

REAL OR FAKE?
Yummy Mummy Surgeries Revealed

Whose got botched boobs?

Wong Is Wrong!
Public hazard threatens Williamses' retirement

Desperate policy wife barters 'no tickets' in exchange for friendship

$2.00

June 5, 2015

CHAPTER 1

MY NAME IS AMIAH JANE WILLIAMS. AMIAH TO MY FRIENDS in Vancouver, Miss Williams at work, AJ to my redneck cousins, and just plain Miah in Kingsley. That's where I was headed at the start of this story. Hardly newsworthy, you would think.

Kingsley, Alberta, population 1431. Home of the Knights, my high school insignia and my parents' before. The large green road sign in the ditch read **Kingsley 27 km, Edmonton 176 km**. I was almost home. Two years had passed since I ran away to Vancouver, yet Kingsley was somehow still home.

Beautiful British Columbia, as that province's licence plates boasted, and the Rocky Mountains were behind me. Ahead was the largely ironed province of Saskatchewan with fields and sky as far as the eye could see. I was back in central Alberta with hills, curves, trees, and a beauty all its own. In early summer, the fields were as thin as Dad's hair, but time would turn them gold, purple, and the brightest yellow imaginable. Wheat, alfalfa, and canola. The countryside was dotted with pumpjacks, great iron horses lifting and bowing their heads, slow and steady, pulling oil from the ground. I passed a service rig, which would be replaced by a pumpjack one day, too.

My driver-side window was rolled down. Sunglasses shielded my eyes from loose strands of shoulder-length, salon-highlighted hair whipping in the wind and me from my eyes in the rear-view mirror. The radio was cranked. Whenever an announcer interrupted the music, I changed the station. Whenever a thought made me anxious, I turned up the volume. The old speakers rattled in protest. I sang along, making up or humming over the words I didn't know. Country, rock, pop ... it didn't matter. I simply refused to think about where I was going or what could be dredged up by going there.

Our first real vacation since we went to Disneyland when I was ten was supposed to be two weeks in a rented chateau walking distance from the Radium Hot Springs, courtesy of Mom and Dad. Instead, Dad had broken his leg. I had expected my parents to make an excuse to cancel the trip, but I couldn't say Dad would go as far as faking surgery. So I had purged my apartment of anything that would rot, reminded my closest friend Nathan to pick up my mail, and drove over twelve hundred kilometres in my rusty '99 Jeep to spend my vacation in Kingsley. My only stops had been for fuel and the most uncomfortable five-hour sleep of my life. Driving was cheaper than flying, though, and I had time, not money.

I had an indefinite amount of time, actually. Nobody except Nathan knew I had recently been fired from my waitressing job at Café des Amis, a pretentious bistro in downtown Vancouver. The first plate I had dropped in weeks landed in the lap of a high-maintenance blonde wearing a baby-blue spring dress. Unfortunately, she had ordered a red wine vinaigrette and also happened to be the owner's niece.

I told myself that after two years of general studies at the University of British Columbia I needed a job in my field anyway. The problem was I was having trouble committing to a major. Before leaving for Kingsley, I had sent out a dozen resumes. For office admin positions that paid well. To be a florist, an event planner, or a grade school tutor, jobs with which I had little or no experience but all sounded fun. And at some restaurants for safe measure. Apparently I needed certification to work for the Happy Camper Preschool. My cell phone remained silent in the cup holder.

The farm—everyone called their farm "the farm"— wasn't far from town. Half an hour by bicycle, five minutes by car. With Kingsley in sight, I turned off the highway onto the gravel, catching my red notebook before it slid off the passenger seat.

Dust billowed into the Jeep. "Shit."

I cranked up my window. The town was probably buzzing with complaints about drought. Farmers liked to complain no matter how good the crop or beef prices. Not my dad, though. "Griping's no rain dance," he would say. Ray Williams always had a better way to spend his time with fences to mend and animals to tend. He liked to be busy. No wonder Mom was stressed. Dad was couchridden and there was no hockey on TV.

I switched off the radio as I turned into the long driveway lined with a split rail fence and Swedish aspens. All led to my childhood home, a movie-worthy red ranch house with a wraparound porch. Duke and Earl greeted me first, running and barking playfully alongside my Jeep as I crept closer to the house. Then I spotted Mom sitting on the porch steps as if waiting for me.

Mom and I were about the same height with the same build and the same oval faces that crinkled when we smiled. There was something Mom had that I didn't, though, something that drew people to her while I remained invisible. My heartstrings tugged at the sight of her. At twenty-five years old, I needed her more than ever, though I never would have admitted it.

"Hey, stranger!" Mom said. "We weren't expecting you until late."

The last we had seen each other was Christmas. I hadn't gone home for Easter break. I had used homework as an excuse, but actually spent the break with some guy named Winston. Purple skinny jeans, two eyebrow rings, barely-lasted-a-month Winston. My parents hadn't come to visit me either. They had been busy with the tail end of calving and the start of seeding. My parents were as likely to visit Vancouver as Winston was Kingsley. I hadn't mentioned the farm would survive a few days without them, and Mom hadn't mentioned she suspected I didn't want to come home.

"How's Dad?"

"He finally fell asleep. The painkillers make him drowsy and a little loopy." Mom whirled her finger around her ear. We laughed, our faces crinkling.

"Let him sleep. I'll still be here when he wakes up."

"Okay. We'll have coffee. Are you hungry? I can make you something to eat."

"I'm okay, Mom. I'm here to help you."

CHAPTER 2

THE RANCH HOUSE HADN'T CHANGED MUCH SINCE I WAS A KID. Inside there was a fresh coat of paint in a slightly different shade of neutral, and the odd knickknack had been added to the homey clutter. I followed Mom to the kitchen. The fridge was a collage of photos, greeting cards, drawings from other people's grandkids, and postcards of Palm Springs from semi-retired friends who actually took vacations. I sat at the oak kitchen table while Mom busied herself making coffee.

The bold red masthead of the *Kingsley Inquirer* stuck out among the bills, flyers, and knitting. I glanced at Mom's back and then carefully pulled the newspaper free. The *Inquirer* looked typical of Hollywood, not small-town Alberta. Sensationalized snapshots and headlines in a variety of sizes covered the front page. The main headline read **Trula Discovers Roland's Online Dating Account!**

The large bold letters were printed across a grainy candid shot of Trula, my former babysitter. Her expression implied that the camera had caught the moment of the scandalous discovery. She wasn't perfectly manicured and posed like in the photo on Mom's fridge, the photo with smiling husband Roland and their two blond kids.

"That's the tabloid I told you about," Mom said. "It's just a no-good rag that stirs up trouble."

"It's not that bad," I said. I laughed. Mom didn't. "Well, why do you pick it up, then?"

"I buy it. A toonie in Kingsley! I'd bet the farm that old Jack Whitby didn't expect this drivel when he retired the *Gazette*, which, by the way, was free like a community newsletter should be."

'*$2.00*' was printed in the bottom right-hand corner below the Friday release date on the front page.

"Why buy it, then?" I corrected myself.

"Because."

"Because" was Mom's cop-out response. I decided she was simply as nosy as everyone else who bought the *Inquirer*. I looked at the cover again. On the right were close-ups of three women in tight shirts with their faces blurred beyond recognition. The headline read **Real or Fake? Yummy Mummy Surgeries Revealed.**

Who wouldn't be curious who in town had paid for breast implants? I thought if these women didn't want the attention, they wouldn't have gotten implants. Mom set a cup of coffee in front of me and sat down with a sigh.

"Thanks," I said, pushing the paper aside.

"Page six."

Apparently, we weren't done. I pulled the paper back and turned to page six.

WONG IS WRONG!

Paying customer of Kingsley Grocery Ray Williams will undergo life-threatening surgery after a catastrophic fall that may lead to an ugly lawsuit.

'He would have the right mind to sue,' a close family friend tells the *Inquirer*.

On Wednesday, June 3rd, Ray careened down the front steps at Kingsley Grocery while carrying a case of bottled water and a bag of apples. His wife Judith was frantic at the scene. So much so, the paramedics took her in the ambulance too!

Ray tried to catch himself, but there was no railing. A local building inspector confirms that store owner Juan Wong, who called the ambulance and gathered the runaway apples, is violating codes and endangering the public.

Suffering a compound fracture to his right leg, Ray could be confined to a wheelchair for up to eight weeks! Sources reveal the ambulance bill alone was $720 and prescription bills are mounting!

Our insider added: 'On the verge of retirement, the Williamses will need all the help they can get.'

"No one said anything about suing," Mom said once I was finished reading the article. "We've been too busy to even think about such things. And I acted perfectly fine considering my husband was moaning like a heifer calving, lying on the sidewalk with his leg bent in unnatural ways."

I had to stop myself from laughing. The way she put it would have been perfect for the *Inquirer.*

"So, who *is* going to help with the fields?" I asked.

"Travis has an extra hand," she said, waving off the subject. Travis was the neighbouring cattle farmer, the son of the former neighbouring cattle farmer. "He's coming over to talk to your dad this afternoon."

On my third trip to my Jeep, I heard the rumble of exhaust and saw a cloud of dust chasing a pickup truck toward the house. Travis, I assumed. I lifted the hatchback and reached for my big suitcase, forgetting how heavy it was. Using the same ratty luggage, I had left Kingsley with less than I had brought back for this vacation. The suitcase crashed to the ground, jerking my arm. A truck door slammed behind me, confirming I had a witness. I smiled at myself, about to make a joke of it before Travis could. He had always had a great sense of humour.

"Need a hand with that?"

I froze. It wasn't Travis. Travis's extra hand was his younger brother, Mike. I turned around slowly. Mike was wearing a white t-shirt, blue jeans, and a ball cap. He leaned against his nineteen-eighty-something single cab Ford pickup with a self-assured smirk on his face. Dammit, he looked like a model posing for a Coca-Cola advertisement. And, dammit, I noticed. I also noticed that after two days of driving, I wasn't looking so good myself. I glanced down at my UBC t-shirt and yoga pants. There was a yellow stain on my shirt. Mustard? I hadn't eaten anything with mustard on it.

A memory so vivid struck me, I could have been seventeen again.

"Miah Williams! How's it going?" Mike called, hanging out the driver-side window of his pickup truck. I was standing in front of Kingsley High. Four years older than me, Mike had already graduated, and before this moment, I couldn't tell if he knew I existed. Not even when I had worn that lime-green string bikini that would've made my dad blush to the dugout where all the Kingsley teens went swimming. My name on his lips made my insides flutter. I didn't wonder why he had nothing better to do on a weekday afternoon, like work. No, I hoped my ponytail was straight. I crossed and uncrossed my arms and tried to make covering the ginormous pimple on my jawline look natural. Mike Hayes had singled me out. It was a dream come true.

"Hi." My voice literally squeaked. I was mortified.

He grinned, well aware of his effect on any girl within a two-town radius. Danika and I had been crushing on him since junior high, and that day of all days she had an orthodontist appointment in the city.

"Stuck on the grad committee?"

"No."

"Avoided that drama trap, eh?"

"Yeah."

"Do you have a date?"

"No." I realized I hadn't answered with more than one syllable and added, "Not yet. Haven't really thought about it." That was a lie. I had been having a recurring nightmare in which my cousin Donny, wearing his dad's powder-blue suit, hands me a corsage. I had even considered being 'too sick' to go, but felt guilty after the three hundred dollars Mom had dropped on my puffy pink princess dress to match Danika's puffy pink princess dress.

"A good-looking girl like you? Really?" Mike asked.

"Well, how about me? I clean up real nice."

I felt like the luckiest girl in Kingsley.

I could have been seventeen again, except I wasn't. The familiar pickup truck was now rusted along the wheel wells and hood, no longer a prized possession but a farm truck. Mike was thicker and not as baby smooth. My stomach twisted for different reasons than it had all those years ago.

"I've never known you to be quiet for so long," he said.

"You don't know me, Michael Elliot Hayes."

"Not my middle name, too? Am I in trouble? Only you and my mother can instill fear in me with just three little words."

I rolled my eyes.

"It's been awhile, Miah," Mike said, turning serious.

I righted my suitcase, fighting the urge to run to my old bedroom. Better yet, to run back to Vancouver. His hand brushed mine as he took the handle. I jerked away, though he pretended not to notice. Did he recognize the ratty luggage? It was technically his. The weight of it didn't slow him down. Empty-handed and feeling foolish, I followed him to the house from which he had once been banned. He knocked a pattern—*rat-a-tat-tat*—on the doorframe before stepping inside.

Mom had some explaining to do.

CHAPTER 3

MIKE SLID OFF HIS WORK BOOTS AND STARTED OFF WITH MY SUITCASE.

"Down the hall, it's the—"

"—second door on the left." He winked over his shoulder. "I remember."

Annoyed and uncomfortable, I kicked off my sandals and followed him to my old bedroom. Inside was a wrought-iron bed covered with a purple patchwork quilt my mom had sewn and a big window with matching curtains. I found the childish treasures—a framed elementary award for being 'most thoughtful,' a poster of a forgotten boy band, teen vampire romance books—a little embarrassing. It appeared as though Mom had made the bed after I had left for school as usual ... seven years ago. She hadn't changed a thing. Not after our big fight when I announced I was moving in with Mike. Not even after I had left Kingsley without telling anyone. I suppose my parents hadn't needed the space. Visions of a big, happy family had inspired the blueprints for the five-bedroom ranch house. After years of trying, my parents had their miracle baby: me. Just me. Some miracle.

Mike set the suitcase down beside the rest of my luggage, where his eyes lingered a beat. My backpack and three ratty suitcases were lined up like Russian nesting dolls.

"Moving back?" Mike asked.

My mind raced through the things I could say and the reasons I couldn't just as quickly. He was baiting me, and I wasn't going to fall for it. Mike shrugged and crossed the room to the big window. He pulled up on the sill, and the window opened an inch. Not locked. I could see his lips curl up at that. He had entered through that window more often than the front door.

"So *you're* going to help my dad?"

"Unless you learned to operate a tractor since you left me."

Mike shut the window a little harder than necessary. The *thud* made me jump. Then he turned to face me, leaning against the dresser. He opened his mouth to say something else, something I'm sure I didn't want to hear, but his eyes flicked over my shoulder and he stopped. My mom was standing in the doorway.

"Miah's a city girl now," she said.

"Hi, Judith. How's it going today?" he asked.

"Oh, we're surviving," she replied.

"Judith?" I repeated.

They looked at me as if *I* was the one acting crazy. As if *I* didn't belong.

"That is my name. You don't expect him to call me Mrs. Williams still, do you?" Mom laughed. "He's almost thirty, not a kid anymore."

"*Almost* thirty, Mrs. Williams," said Mike. "Almost."

"Oh, as if thirty is old." Mom swatted the air between them. She was acting the way I remembered women acting around Mike. Other women, not my mom.

"Thirty may not be old, but I'm not ready for it yet."

The disturbing scene was interrupted by a succession of thuds, a muffled *dammit*, and running water from the bathroom across the hall.

"Oh, Ray!" Mom remembered why she was there. She clearly hadn't come to rescue me, her daughter. Mike and I followed her to the hall, where I deliberately stood so Mom was between us. She knocked on the bathroom door. "Do you need a hand in there?"

"I've got two hands. It's a leg I need," Dad grumbled. "Don't know what you suppose you could help with in here."

The door opened inward. There was nothing someone from the outside could do to help with the wheelchair in the way, but that didn't stop Mom from hovering. She guided the door on its fixed path. Once Dad had manoeuvred himself to sit in the open doorway, he spotted me.

"There's my girl!"

Dad's leg was wrapped in bandages and propped up on a wheelchair attachment. Dried blood darkened the area where the incisions were buried. Surgery had been a couple of days ago. Should there have been blood on the bandages? Shouldn't his leg have been in a cast? I had expected hard plaster I could sign with Xs and Os like a sixth grader. I knew Dad's leg would heal. He might walk with a limp, but he would walk. It was just that his face was so pale, his already wiry frame leaner. Slim and five foot nine, Dad had never looked big but had always been tough. Suddenly he seemed softer, wrinklier, greyer. I told myself the sudden urge to cry was from the two days of driving, the pressure of having no job, and the tension of being within Mike's reach, on top of borrowed stress from my mom. I fooled no one. I swallowed the lump in my throat and forced a smile on my face a moment too late.

"Hi, Dad," I said.

"Don't look at me like that. It's just a broken bone."

"You're going to hurt the man's pride," said Mike.

Dad's gaze levelled on Mike, who was leaning against the doorframe of my old bedroom. "Well, look what the cat dragged in."

A memory that had been safely buried made my stomach twist a little more. It had happened about six months after I had moved out.

I burst through the front door of the red ranch house with mascara burning my eyes. Mom and Dad were on the couch, watching the Weather Channel. They were content watching the damn weatherman on a Friday night! My sudden appearance rendered them momentarily speechless. Sobbing, I threw myself onto the couch and buried my head in my mom's shoulder. Then Mike's headlights flooded the living room.

"Make him go away!" I cried.

Dad reached the front porch with his shotgun before Mike's boots touched the ground.

"You've got about thirty seconds to convince me not to shoot," Dad called.

I had gone back to Mike a couple days later. I just overreacted, I insisted as much to myself as anyone. That hadn't fooled my parents, at first anyway. Mike had been banned.

This time Dad didn't have a shotgun in his hand. He seemed happy to see Mike and to escape this awkward moment with his daughter.

"Heard someone might need an extra leg around here," Mike said.

"You're just after more banana bread," Dad replied.

Mom started pushing Dad's wheelchair down the hall, and Mike followed. I remained rooted in the hallway mumbling something lame about needing to unpack, but no one seemed to notice.

"You know better if you're after banana bread," Mom told Mike as they rounded the corner to the kitchen. "I pick up the ingredients on Friday. Overripe bananas are Kingsley Grocery's specialty."

CHAPTER 4

MOM HADN'T BEEN KIDDING ABOUT DAD'S MEDICATION making him loopy. After he wasted his energy discussing chores and NHL draft picks with Mike, instead of visiting the daughter he hadn't seen for over six months, he swallowed a couple of white pills for dinner. In less than twenty minutes, he was softly singing an old Waylon Jennings song. Mom helped him onto the couch and propped his leg on two pillows. When she finally stepped away from her drowsy patient and his over-fluffed pillows, I followed her to the kitchen.

"How can I help?"

"Just relax. You're on vacation. Why don't you give Danika a call?"

"No, I came to help."

She went to the sink of dirty dishes and put her hand on the tap, but she stopped to stare out the window where the sun hung low over the fields.

"He can't get comfortable, but he's not the only one," she said. Her whole body seemed to slump. "I'm scared I'll bump him in the night, but I can't sleep somewhere else. Instead of calling out, the stubborn man will hurt himself trying to get out of bed on his own. I'm exhausted."

"You need one of those video baby monitors," I said. At least she was smiling when she turned to face me. "Let me help."

"Okay. You want to help? Keep an eye on your father while I take a nap."

Mom's slippers made scuffing noises on the hardwood to her bedroom. An hour later, the supper dishes were drying and a news broadcast flickered on the muted TV while Mom, Dad, and the dogs slept. There was no one else around for a mile in any direction. The only sound was the loud tick of the grand-father clock in the corner, like time methodically poking me with its finger. I missed the traffic noise of the city and even the fat, hairy guy stomping in the upstairs apartment. Quiet country nights had once made me feel at peace but now felt ominous. When had it changed? I knew. It had changed when everything else had changed.

Dad coughed and shifted on the couch.

"Miah?"

"Here, Dad. Do you have the remote?" I needed the noise of the TV.

"Don't forget, Miah," he said, his eyes wide and glassy. Loopy. "Don't forget the list."

"Okay, I won't. Where's the remote?"

"It's in the top left-hand drawer of the toolbox."

"What?"

"The wolf list. It's the key to keeping the farm running. Without the list, if we don't do the things on the list, it's over. All over. The wolf is howling at our door."

Dad's eyes closed. Soon he was snoring. Even asleep and high on prescription drugs he looked like he was in pain. I looked all around the couch but suspected the remote was underneath him somewhere. My parents had only basic cable anyway. They couldn't be bothered with any technology that wasn't sold at John Deere. Their shared cell phone flipped open. Downloads and apps were to my parents like castrating and swathers to my friends in Vancouver.

I wished I hadn't forgotten to bring my latest piece of research for narrowing down my major. I could picture it on the kitchen counter in my one-bedroom apartment. Not another dreary textbook but a novel about a badass heroine challenging a corrupt multi-million-dollar company only a year after passing the bar. I was on Chapter 4 and already suspected corporate law was too intense for me, but the plot was entertaining.

I thought it safe to slip into the study—one of the ranch house's unneeded bedrooms—for something to read. The bookshelf was crammed with more knickknacks and photo albums than books. My eyes caught on a framed photo from my graduation banquet. Danika, her escort, me, and Mike. The only one in the picture I didn't mind the sight of was Danika's date, geeky what's-his-name. I looked like cotton candy with curls and a tiara. I pushed the picture over, the cheap frame clattering against the shelf.

I wasn't in the mood for one of Mom's historical romance novels or one of Dad's sports hero autobiographies. Instead, I discovered a neat stack of the *Inquirer*.

Dad was in the same position on the couch as I had left him. I settled back into the recliner and opened the first issue. The content was newsworthy as far as small-town news went, but written in a more entertaining way. Better than the *Gazette*'s ever-cheerful small-town drivel. I hadn't meant to fall asleep.

"What are you doing?" Mom exclaimed. I bolted upright, sending the *Inquirers* from my lap to the floor. It took me a second to realize she wasn't talking to me. Dad was crumpled on the floor, trying with both hands to lift his injured leg, which was twisted and caught between the couch cushions. His face was contorted and flushed, and his breath hissed between clenched teeth.

"Oh, Dad!"

I took two steps toward him, but Mom held up her hand as if to say *Never mind* and set to helping Dad into his wheelchair.

"Why didn't you ask for help? I knew I shouldn't have

gone to bed," she said as she hooked her hands under his armpits and heaved. She got him high enough that his injured leg came out from between the cushions at the same time as his backside slid into the seat of his wheelchair.

"I just need to take a leak," he grumbled.

CHAPTER 5

DAYS STARTED EARLY ON THE FARM, EVEN WHEN THE FARMER was broken.

"Why didn't you wake me?" I sounded like a sulky teenager. I was tired and still felt guilty about falling asleep the night I had returned to Kingsley. Ever since, all I had done was read old issues of the *Inquirer*, write in my red notebook, and uselessly follow Mom around.

"Why would I? You're on vacation," Mom said, sipping her coffee.

"This *is* early for my girl," Dad said.

It wasn't even seven a.m. From my elementary to university years, my alarm barely allowed time to get to school. In high school, the girls in my class had awoken at dawn to iron their hair and plaster on makeup. My ponytail, mascara, and lip gloss were enough for me if it meant an extra hour of sleep.

I sat beside Dad and eyed his untouched oatmeal. I was glad to see him lucid, but the depth of his frown lines and the dark circles under his eyes showed the price he paid.

"I used to help out around here as a kid."

"You followed your dad around after school, if it suited your fancy and the weather was right. Ray wakes the rooster half the time."

We never had a rooster. We had a grain farm and raised a hundred fifty head of cattle at most.

"I fed the cats," I said. Most farm kids didn't get off so easily. "And I do have eight o'clock classes, you know." Actually, I had only ever had one for one semester, and only because I had slept in and missed pre-registration for a mandatory English course. I would have rather taken Japanese at night.

"It was my choice for life, not yours," Dad said.

"Ha! What about me then?" Mom asked. "I recall getting up with the rooster every morning to make breakfast, pack lunches, and feed those damn cats."

Dad twisted the childproof cap off one of five pill bottles on the kitchen table. He washed a blue antibiotic down with a sip of water, grinning over the glass at Mom. "You signed the marriage contract."

"There seems to have been a lot of fine print in that contract," Mom said. She patted his hand on the table where the light glinted off her wedding set. She was also wearing her watch and a pair of gold earrings. Dad wasn't wearing Wranglers because of his leg, but he had on a clean pair of sweatpants. No rips or flannel with checked patterns on either of them.

"Where are we going?" I asked.

"Your dad has an appointment with the specialist. Hopefully his little fall the other night didn't tear anything."

Mom stood to put her breakfast dishes in the sink. When her back was turned, Dad slid his oatmeal toward me. There was no sense in it going to waste. As I took a bite, I wondered if I had time for a quick shower before we left.

"I was thinking, if you have time, you could run some errands in town while your dad and I are gone," Mom said.

What? Before I could swallow my bite of oatmeal and

respond, there was a knock on the front door. A *rat-a-tat-tat* leaving no doubt as to who had arrived. I felt like I had been slapped twice. Neither of my parents made eye contact with me before Mike was standing in the kitchen.

"What's on the agenda today, Boss?"

"They're going to a specialist appointment," I said.

"I know. I meant what's on *my* agenda. I work here, remember?" Mike gave me another one of those annoying winks. "You're up early. Not feeling well?"

"I'm fine. Just leave the errand list on the table, Mom," I said, retreating from the kitchen before anyone could see my burning face or watering eyes. Let Mike finish the damn oatmeal. I didn't have much of an appetite anymore.

Everyone was gone by the time I re-emerged from my extra-long hot shower. I stalled some more by looking for ways to be useful around the house that Mom kept saying was 'filthy.' It looked fine to me. I would have probably cleaned it wrong anyway. I wasn't ready to face town, but I reached for my keys and Mom's errand list.

Welcome to Kingsley, where little has changed since 1953. Okay, the big wooden sign didn't actually say that last part. I turned off the highway, passing the truck stop. Most travellers only knew Kingsley for the truck stop. The attached Minimart was new. Big year for the town, 2013. I had moved out, and the Minimart had moved in.

A couple dozen cars and a few bicycles were parked on Main Street. The hotel bar at one end was filled with old men discussing the prairie farm report and oil prices. The café at the other end was filled with grey-haired women complaining about the old men. In between, on either side of the road, were a bunch of little shops and offices: a hardware store, a gift shop, a hair salon, a pharmacy, and so on.

I picked up the dog food from the vet clinic and the mail from the post office. Next on the list was a mystery novel for Dad. He wasn't going to read it. The dreams he was having from those pills were probably twice as entertaining. Mom just wanted me to go to the library. Danika worked at the library.

Danika Rooker—now Mrs. RC Miller—and I had become

best friends as soon as the teacher sat us side by side at the blue table on our first day of kindergarten. We had bonded over our matching pink dresses—so, basically over the fact that her baba and my mom shopped at the same department store. Three years ago, I had been the maid of honour at Danika's wedding. Now, Danika was a Facebook friend. We exchanged likes on status updates and posts on birthdays.

Through the small square pane of glass in the library door I could see her. Barely five feet tall, she had bleached-blonde hair, manicured nails, and makeup like she was waiting to be discovered at any moment. We used to call her curvaceous, but now pudgy was a more accurate description. I thought of the cover of the previous week's *Inquirer* and wondered if Danika was another yummy mummy who had paid to increase her cup size. Her chest was comparable to my backside in a push-up bra.

Danika was busy with something on the counter and had twisted to talk to someone I couldn't see. I took a deep breath, about to enter an abandoned warzone filled with landmines.

CHAPTER 6

THE CHIMES ABOVE THE DOOR MADE DANIKA GASP AND HIDE whatever she was working on.

"Well, alert the paper, it's Miah! I heard you were back in town, but now I actually believe it," she said, returning a dinosaur picture book and a roll of Scotch Tape to the counter. She flashed a row of perfectly straight white teeth. Her orthodontist deserved an award. I forced a smile to match hers in size and lack of sincerity. I felt like I had stepped on one of those landmines and was slowly easing my foot off, hoping it wasn't live.

"Who is it, Mommy?" A voice came from behind the counter and had me curious to see the owner, but he was too short to be seen from the door.

"Back to timeout, Benton. Five minutes, remember? No ripping library books!" She rolled her eyes at me in a conspiratorial way. "You almost gave me a heart attack. I thought you were my boss. It's just not my day. Two books ruined. I spilt breast milk on the other."

I wasn't sure she needed to specify the type of milk rippling the pages of the *Silly Nursery Rhymes* book she held up as proof, but it explained her overly full V-neck.

"If you put the book under something heavy in the freezer, it will smooth out the pages," I said, pushing down the painful reminder that when Mom had called to lecture me for not telling her Danika was pregnant again—*Imagine how silly I felt when Betty brought it up at the diner,* she had said—I had to pretend it had merely slipped my mind. Imagine how silly *I* had felt. The only birth announcement I had received was a public social media post.

"Really?"

"I dropped my anthropology textbook in the bath last semester. The freezer trick worked for me."

All Danika heard was *book* and *freezer*. Or at least that was all she cared about. She quickly disappeared into the back room. I approached the counter, and Benton peeked one chocolate-coloured eye over his shoulder at me. He had a mess of brown curls and was wearing the cutest denim overalls. I wiggled my fingers at him, and he shoved his nose back in the corner. Moments later, Danika reappeared carrying a pink bundle. Benton hadn't been much older than that when I had left Kingsley.

"She's so tiny," I said.

"You've obviously never had a baby. Abigail was eight pounds, seven ounces when she was born. You are my chunky monkey, aren't you?" she cooed.

"My baby," Benton announced. Abandoning his timeout, he climbed onto a chair so his head was higher than the counter.

I had mixed feelings seeing the happy little family. The plan had always been to be in each other's weddings, buy our kids matching pink dresses, and live next door to each other in cute little houses surrounded by white picket fences. Now Danika was freezing picture books and I, textbooks.

"I'm here because of Dad's accident," I blurted.

"I figured. I called your mom as soon as I heard, but everyone in town has read about it in the paper. Have you seen it yet?"

"The *Kingsley Inquirer*? Yeah," I said, quickly adding, "I've been reading through some of Mom's old issues."

"The *Gazette* disappeared and—ta-da!—the *Inquirer.* No one knows where it comes from. Kingsley Grocery is the only store that sells it, though."

"Sounds convenient."

"You're not the first to say so, but I doubt Mr. Wong has a firm enough grasp on the English language to manage the *Inquirer*'s sarcasm." Suddenly her face lit up, and it was like she was talking to someone who wasn't me. "Oh my gosh, did you see the article about Trula and Roland? Her daughter Kenzie babysat Benton once. I heard Roland is sleeping on his mom's couch. I wonder which website he was on. I bet it was one of those dirty hook-up ones."

"You always liked a good story."

Danika shrugged.

"Baba doesn't allow the *Inquirer* in the house," she said, shifting into an impression of her eighty-some-year-old grandmother. "'You buy that paper and people wonder. They want to know what you're thinking and what you're saying. In my day, your business was no one else's business.'"

I laughed. With a small ache in my chest, I realized again how much I had missed Danika.

"That's Baba!" Benton said, looking up from the plastic dinosaurs he was lining up on the floor.

"No, no. Mommy is just being silly. Never mind grown-up talk and play with your dinosaurs." She turned her attention back to me. "Some people refuse to buy the *Inquirer*, but I think it's great. When Benton was terrified of monsters under his bed, I wrote to *Dear Deirdre*. She actually had good advice: Monster Go Away Spray. And, since Benton agrees with Mommy that it's better to be safe than sorry, RC now deodorizes the entire upstairs every night. Win–win for me."

The chimes above the door announced a pimply teenager with headphones. He needed to sign in to use one of the public computers. Danika looked around her for a place to set the baby before plunking her in my arms and leading the teenager to the computer stations. I couldn't hear what they were talking about and couldn't see what she was typing, but they were taking turns on the keyboard. Abby sucked her bottom lip in her sleep, oblivious to the fact that a complete stranger was holding her. Together, we located the bookshelf deemed the Mystery section and chose three novels, each by a different king of the bestsellers list. Danika was back at the counter when we returned.

"When do you go back? I'm assuming you're going back," she said.

"Yeah, I have to get ready for school: sort my classes, do a bunch of readings, check in with my professors." The last part wasn't really a thing, but it sounded important and talking to at least a guidance counsellor probably wasn't a bad idea. "I leave next weekend."

"That's too bad. There's a bonfire at the creek for the Canada Day fireworks. Would have been like the good ol' days, but you'll be gone by then," Danika said as she scanned the books into the library computer, presumably under Mom's account.

"Yeah, the good ol' days," I repeated. The pimply teenager had broken the spell. It was awkward between us again. Abigail started to fuss, and Danika immediately traded her for the novels. "Well, I had better get to the grocery store. Mom has a list of stuff she wants me to pick up."

"Be a dear and grab me a copy of the *Inquirer* while you're there? I need something to read," Danika said.

With a sweep of my hand, I gestured to the shelves of books around her.

"I've read them all."

"Right," I said, doubtfully, and she flashed those perfect teeth at me again.

A piece of paper reading *Watch Your Step* was taped to the front door of Kingsley Grocery. The store was surprisingly busy. I couldn't help wondering if someone was lurking in the cereal aisle, waiting for a chance to slip a note into the locked contributions box on the counter. The inside page of every issue clearly stated that stories and tips were welcome through either the contributions box at Kingsley Grocery or theinquirer@freemail.com.

An Asian man, whom I presumed was Mr. Wong, worked the cash register. The Wongs had bought the store last year. Kingsley Grocery changed hands frequently. Mr. Wong nodded in my direction. I picked up a red plastic basket from the stack beside the door. Then I collected the eggs, chocolate chips, and bananas on Mom's list.

"Hello," I said, when it was my turn at the till.

Mr. Wong put the bananas on the scale. They were overripe, but I would be paying full price.

"You must be Mrs. Williams's daughter. Banana bread every other week. And ..." he motioned toward the newspaper stand.

"Thanks for reminding me," I said, choosing two copies of the *Inquirer* from the stack and putting four dollars in the contributions box.

"Do you publish the paper?" I asked. I couldn't help myself. I wanted to see what he would say. Did I imagine the ears of the woman beside me perking?

"No, no. I only put in the coupons to help business. See?" He flipped to the coupons and jabbed the paper a couple times with his finger. "Your mother says she buys the paper for the coupons."

Spending two dollars on a newspaper for fifty cents off a can of ketchup didn't add up, but saying so would have felt disloyal. Under Mr. Wong's watchful eye, I added a can of ketchup to my purchases.

"And you can tell your father there will be no more falls," Mr. Wong said, pointing through the glass at the shiny new handrail I hadn't noticed on my way in. See, some good came from the paper. No more falls.

I cut across the street to give Danika her copy of the *Inquirer*. Then I hopped into my Jeep, put the groceries on the passenger seat, and started for the farm. My visit into Kingsley hadn't been so bad after all. I had already driven halfway down the block when I glanced over and the smallest headline in the bottom left-hand corner on the cover of the *Inquirer* caught my eye. **'I was going to propose': Heartbroken Mike Hayes Tells All**

KINGSLEY INQUIRER

5 TIPS FOR DIABETIC-FRIENDLY BAKING

$2-MILLION DOLLAR DIVORCE

TRULA WANTS THE HOUSE
ROLAND WANTS HIS FAMILY BACK

EXCLUSIVE:
Cancer battle from the front lines

• Local fundraiser raises $6,270
• The latest prognosis
• Doctors tell Gladys to get her affairs in order

'I was going to propose'
Heartbroken Mike Hayes Tells All

DROUGHT!
Rain Dancers Wanted

$2.00
June 19, 2015

CHAPTER 7

"WHAT!" I GRABBED FOR THE *INQUIRER* FROM THE PASSENGER SEAT, causing my Jeep to swerve toward oncoming traffic—the only other moving vehicle on Main Street. The other driver laid on the horn of his black jacked-up truck. Every second vehicle in rural Alberta was black and jacked-up. I dropped the *Inquirer* and swerved back onto my side of the road. Driving 30 km/h gave the other driver plenty of time to express himself with obscene hand gestures as we passed. Since I had nearly caused a car wreck in downtown Kingsley, I kept my eyes on the road the rest of the way to the farm. By the time I had parked next to Mom's empty space, I was in dire need of an antacid.

I flipped quickly through the tabloid but missed the article and had to start again. Then there it was, short and far from sweet.

MIKE HAYES'S HEARTBREAK
Miah's back ... but not for him

What Mike Hayes thought was forever ended before it started when Miah Williams, live-in girlfriend of four years, ran off in the dark of night without telling anyone!

'Mike came home from work one day to find half his stuff gone,' a mutual friend reveals to the *Inquirer*. 'Mike was devastated. He was going to propose.'

The breakup initiated a string of bad luck for Mike. Shortly after Miah split, Mike was fired from his job at Trenton Auto Body, his dad suffered a stroke, and his dog Rex was hit by a car. Despite hard times, rumour has it Mike can't bring himself to sell the engagement ring Miah never knew about.

It was no secret in Kingsley that Miah's parents, Ray and Judith Williams, weren't Mike's biggest fans. But while Miah has been building a new life in the big city of Vancouver, Mike has been mending fences with his former in-laws by mending fences on the Williams farm.

Locals are hopeful Miah's moral support will encourage her dad to a speedy recovery after his catastrophic fall at Kingsley Grocery, but some can't help but wonder how long they will be graced with her presence. Is Miah too good for her roots? Or is there more to this tale than meets the eye?

'The girl next door and the hometown stud, they were an odd match from the start,' says a teacher from their former high school. 'I never believed the perfect front, myself.'

I immediately dialled Nathan on my cell phone. Voicemail.

"We need to talk," I said before hanging up.

I needed to calm down. What did the article say exactly? I was home because of Dad's surgery. True. I had run away from Kingsley. True. Though seeing it in print was uncomfortable. I hadn't taken half of Mike's stuff, but Mike had likely said I did. The *Inquirer* suggested I thought myself too good for the town, but that wasn't true, was it? It also suggested there may have been more to my leaving. Wasn't that what I wished my mom and Danika would see? I reminded myself that having these things printed in plain sight was better than having them whispered behind my back. Yet my skin itched with the need to take action.

I glanced at the barn in my side mirror. With my phone and the tabloid clutched in my hand, I got out of the Jeep, slammed the door, and stormed to the barn. I shoved open the man door, which never latched properly. I was met with a familiar, warm, musty smell. The enormous space held the grain truck, the combine, the seeder, and a couple other miscellaneous contraptions. Tools and supplies were hanging on and stacked against the walls and spewing from cupboards and shelves. My dad's organized chaos. Country music played low on the radio, which hadn't been turned off since before I was born.

"Hey!" I called, anger driving me to the source of this nonsense about an engagement ring. "Mike! Are you in here?"

The only response was from my echo. My shadow stretched before me on the cement floor. I kicked at some bits of straw and slapped the *Inquirer* against the dusty red toolbox. The toolbox was as tall as me and twice as wide as the man door; it reminded me of something. The wolf list. The night Dad had fallen off the couch he had babbled something about an all-important list in the toolbox. The radio protested with static as I started opening and closing drawers, interrupting the cowboy's summer tribute to beer drinking. In the top left drawer was a coil notebook with a picture of a lone wolf on the cover. The cover was stained with oil, but the pages looked fairly new.

- *Fix fence on southeast section*
- *Fix latch on barn door*
- *Build grain bins*
- *Clear tree line*
- *Repair cattle waters*
- *Service combine*
- *Service grain truck*
- *Resurrect old red?*
- *Research pesticides*
- *Re-side shop*
- *Paint fence, barn, dog house, etc.*

The list went on for two and a half pages in Dad's neat printing. Two and a half pages of things that needed to be done; otherwise ... what? The wolf? Desperation would have explained why my parents would resort to hiring Mike Hayes. Dad had been behind before he had even broken his leg. Feeling humbled, I replaced the notebook and retreated from the barn.

Mom and Dad still weren't home by the time the banana bread was cooling on the counter and I closed the oven on a tuna casserole. By force of habit, my eyes were drawn to the digital clock on the stove. 4:47. That uncomfortable feeling crept over me again. Supper would be on the table by six.

Working as a floor hand on a service rig, Mike got home and sat at the head of the table. The table was set, complete with napkins and a vase of flowers I had snipped from the neighbour's rose bush that grew into our yard through the slats of the fence. I presented my first ever meatloaf, a treat to celebrate nothing at all.

"It's nice coming home and having supper on the table by six."

It was almost six thirty.

"I usually do have supper on the table by six."

"Usually." Mike smiled. "Get me a beer while you're up, will you?"

The sound of car doors interrupted the memory. I hurried to the porch where I watched. I felt useless as Dad slowly made his way on crutches to the house. Usually Duke and Earl were eager to be pet or play fetch, but even they sensed Dad was miserable and let him be.

"There's my girl," Dad said as I held the front door open for him. Once he had gone inside, I sat next to Mom on the porch steps.

"He needs another surgery, two weeks from today," she said. "It'll be at least another two weeks from there before the doctor will consider a cast. So another month before he can do moderate work."

We sat for a bit. I was thinking about the wolf howling at Dad's door and how little work on the farm was 'moderate.' Mom was probably thinking that this second surgery wouldn't have been necessary if I hadn't fallen asleep the other night. Dad had fallen off the couch because I hadn't been awake to help him.

With a deep breath that seemed like an effort to pull herself together, Mom straightened. "I best be getting something on for supper."

"There's a casserole in the oven."

She smiled. "Thank you."

At least I had done that right. It was a start.

CHAPTER 8

"I'VE BEEN EXPECTING TO HEAR YOUR TIRES TEARING UP THE GRAVEL in the driveway for five days now," Mom said.

"Judith," Dad said in a warning tone.

"What? We agreed no questions. I didn't ask a question," she said. "We've all seen the article in the *Inquirer*. It's silly that we don't talk about it."

We had fallen into a routine since Dad's last appointment, the one that deemed a second surgery necessary and loomed over us all. Mom did the evening chores while I prepared supper, we all ate together, and then Mom and I cleaned up the kitchen while Dad napped on the couch. On good nights, like tonight, he lingered as long as the conversation interested him.

Dad began manoeuvring his wheelchair toward the living room. Mom set down the dishtowel to help. Pillows didn't fluff themselves. Dishes wouldn't wash themselves, either. Nor would food prepare itself, the house straighten itself, the lawn mow itself, or the dogs feed and throw a ball for themselves. These were the simple things I did, that Mom trusted me with so she could take care of Dad. The things on Dad's wolf list also wouldn't do themselves, and I wondered if maybe a closer look would reveal a few I could manage over the next few days.

I went to the table for Dad's coffee cup, but wiped my wet hands on my jeans and picked up the *Inquirer* instead. I flipped to the article: **Mike Hayes's Heartbreak.** I was mesmerized by the picture of the engagement ring, even if the small print below said "representation." The ring Mike had purchased—if he had actually purchased a ring—probably didn't look anything like the one in the picture. The one in the picture looked expensive.

I really needed to talk to Nathan. I had left a second, more urgent voicemail, but still hadn't heard from him. With a sigh, I dropped the *Inquirer* before Mom could catch me reading it.

"All I was getting at was that it has been nice having you home," Mom said as she returned. She picked up the conversation where she had left off as if she hadn't left at all. She lowered her voice. "It's too bad you're leaving in a couple days. Your dad needs you. I mean it," she continued, seeing my doubtful expression. "It's going to be tough the next couple weeks. Travis and Mike are vaccinating their herd and then hauling to pasture. We won't have the extra help with morning chores for awhile."

"Then maybe I should stay a little longer," I said. I don't know who was more surprised, Mom or me.

"Will the bistro give you more days off?"

"The bistro?" Mom assumed I still had a job waiting for me in Vancouver.

"I can call and explain the situation," she offered.

"Oh, no," I said quickly. "I'm pretty sure the bistro won't mind."

"Good, and don't worry about the extra time off financially. We will be paying you for your work here." Mom held up her hand before I could protest. "We know you are determined to make it on your own in the big city, Miss Independent. You would be working hard for the money just like any other hired hand." Mom bumped her elbow against mine in a contrived sort of way. This had been her plan all along, I realized.

I scrubbed another dish, a little harder than necessary, and handed it to her to dry. I didn't like being fed information on a need-to-know basis like a child.

"Speaking of hired hands, how did Mike end up working here?" I asked, risking the fragile peace we had shared since Dad's doctor appointment.

"I've been waiting for that one," she said. For someone who had been expecting the question, she took a long time to answer. "We hired Mike out of respect for Edith and Peter and for business. Your dad has been negotiating with Travis."

Edith and Peter Hayes had three children: Claire, Laura, and Travis. Then eight years later they had a surprise: Mike.

"That's nepotism. And negotiating what?"

"Travis is expanding, and Mike wants in on it. Last fall Travis told Mike he would partner with him on two conditions: he needed to prove for a year that he can stick to something, and he needed to pay for his own cattle."

"Mike's been working here since the fall and you didn't say anything! Wait, I was here for Christmas and you didn't say anything!"

I stopped scrubbing the casserole dish in my hands and glared at Mom's profile. She deliberately kept her eyes on the mixing bowl she was drying.

"Mike was the one who had suggested Travis talk to your dad. The idea was that Mike learns the ropes, earns a bit to cut in his share, and the Hayeses buy us out."

"What? Why? You're trusting Mike!"

"We're trusting Travis. Cattle are a lot of work and prices are really good right now. We're going to turn the pasture into farmland. Your dad and I aren't spring chickens anymore."

With my teeth clenched, I resumed scrubbing the casserole dish. I thought of the wolf howling at Dad's door. I also thought of Mike and his all-too-familiar *rat-a-tat-tat* when he smelled banana bread.

"Maybe Mike has finally found his calling," Mom said. "Before your dad's accident, Mike showed up like clockwork four days a week. And he's been here every morning since the accident. Your dad said all of those odd jobs Mike has had are proving kind of handy."

People see what they want to see. Maybe I would have said as much, but a knock—a normal knock—at the front door interrupted our conversation.

I stayed in the kitchen and put dishes away while Mom answered the door. I assumed she hadn't returned because she was avoiding me, but on my way to the living room I heard that her company hadn't left yet. I recognized the voice immediately and stopped out of sight to listen.

"This is a great idea," Danika said. "I ended up with a second set of baby monitors after Abby was born, so keep this one as long as you need."

"It was Miah's idea," Mom said. "Are you sure you can't come in for a few minutes? She's just in the kitchen."

"No, I'm sorry. Abby and Benton are waiting in the car. It's too bad Miah and I didn't get a chance to really catch up. I invited her to the creek for the Canada Day fireworks, but she's leaving."

"I think she mentioned that," Mom said. I hadn't mentioned it. I had purposely avoided mentioning it. "But it works out perfectly because Miah will be home now."

"Oh?" Danika's obvious lack of enthusiasm stung.

"Yes," Mom pressed, "so you can just pick her up like old times."

They said their friendly goodbyes, and Mom closed the door.

"Judith," Dad said again in the same warning tone he had used in the kitchen.

"Oh, you never mind," she said.

Mom went down the hall and into the bathroom. The path to the recliner was clear. Dad opened one eye to peek at me as I sat down.

"I hear you're staying awhile," he said.

"News travels fast."

Dad smiled. "Good. It's been nice having you home. Your mom needs you. I think she's losing her marbles."

That night, while I lay in the dark, I saw Danika and her happy little family at the library. I saw Mom and Dad flirting at breakfast and having entire conversations with just one look. I saw the beautiful ring in the *Inquirer*. I felt failure. I hadn't cried myself to sleep for months, but that night I did.

CHAPTER 9

I STILL HADN'T HEARD BACK FROM NATHAN. I SENT HIM A TEXT, not expecting a response.

> Are you waiting until I calm down or until I get home?

I was staring at the words I had just written when the blinking '...' appeared. Nathan was writing a response.

> Both
>
> You're going to be waiting a LONG time
>
> What do you mean?

I didn't reply because he didn't deserve a reply, and two minutes later my cell phone started ringing. I accepted the call.

"This better be good."

"Hi, Amiah. I miss you," Nathan said. "You are coming back, aren't you?"

"Should I?"

"Okay, let me explain. We have our rules. Rule one: whatever is in the contributions box is published as long as a) it has a grain of truth and b) it doesn't land us in court, jail, or early graves. Rule two: stay neutral and anonymous. Rule three—"

"I know the rules, Nathan." I was the one who had written the first draft of the rules he was reciting on a cocktail napkin at the Pink Rooster where Nathan bartended. We each had a copy printed, laminated, and hanging on the wall above our desks in our apartments. Everything seemed more official laminated.

"So someone actually put this crap about Mike and an engagement ring in the contributions box?" Again, I imagined someone lurking in the cereal aisle at Kingsley Grocery, waiting for Danika's disapproving Baba to pay for a loaf of bread with the nickels and dimes at the bottom of her gigantic purse so the lie scribbled on a scrap of paper could be slipped into the contributions box. I wanted to know who. And what if it wasn't a lie? I couldn't discuss that with Nathan, though, because that would be admitting that I cared whether it was true or not. Nathan would ask me why I cared, and I didn't know why I cared. I just did.

"Mostly, yes. Twice. So the article had to be written, and obviously I had to be the one to write it." Nathan was right. Not including a story obviously suited for the *Inquirer* would draw unwelcome attention. "But I totally humanized your character by adding the parts about you rushing home to care for your dad and having mysterious reasons for leaving in the first place. The truth always comes out, remember?"

"I could really go for one of your apple martinis right now," I said. I had had several of them the night the *Inquirer* was conceived.

"And," Nathan continued, knowing he was weakening my resolve, "I thought this was the whole point of the *Inquirer*. I mean besides for our own delicious entertainment and to pay back our wretched student loans."

When I had first moved to Vancouver, I had relied on a student loan to pay for my tuition and living expenses. A student loan I had gotten with a signature Mike didn't technically know he had given a week before I had left Kingsley. Nathan and I had just finished paying it off with the *Inquirer* money.

"And the Frappuccinos and movie tickets?"

"Those were occasional rewards for all our hard work giving the *Gazette* a much-needed facelift. Trust me, Amiah."

"Trust isn't in my dictionary," I said, but Nathan had the closest thing to it. "I'm just sticking around here until Dad is in his cast and can manage some of the chores again. Feel free to spell that out, too."

"You're okay then?"

"I have nothing to hide. There's nothing more to write anyway."

"Exactly. So what kind of chores?"

"Tomorrow I'm going to clean stalls."

Nathan burst out laughing. "Your plan for tomorrow is to shovel shit? By George, I reckon that'll be more fun than the Monopoly tournament on the weekend. Don't go mucking up them good overalls now, y'hear?"

As much as I wanted to call him of all people out on stereotypes, Mom appeared at my bedroom door.

"Goodbye, Nathan," I said. He was still laughing at his own joke when I hung up. I was smiling and Mom smiled at that. "What's up?" I asked before she could ask any questions.

Dad was slightly better with technology than Mom, but he had refused to help her spy on him. She enlisted me to set up the video baby monitor Danika had loaned them. At last Mom was willing to leave Dad alone for an hour. Wearing borrowed rubber boots, I clomped alongside her to the pasture for my lesson on morning chores. I didn't have to worry about awkward conversation along the way thanks to Dad. As punishment for invading his privacy, he narrated his every move over the monitor, since we 'were so interested and all.'

"I'm reaching for the remote. I've got the remote. Changing the channel. News. Too depressing. Changing the channel. Toilet paper commercial. The one with the cute fuzzy bear. Now dish soap. Not the stuff we use but the kind that smells like green apples."

"As if he would know," Mom muttered.

"Preseason football panel. Perfect. Let's see how the Eskimos are shaping up this season."

We were powerless to retaliate because, unlike a walkie-talkie, the baby monitor allowed us to hear Dad but he couldn't hear us.

"He does know we can see him, too, right?" I asked.

"Don't look," Dad said. Of course, we looked at the monitor. We had a close-up of his face as he pretended to pick his nose.

"He knows," Mom said.

Luckily, Dad's medication took effect or he got bored. Soon he was snoring so loudly we had to turn the volume down on the monitor to hear each other. Mom started by explaining the importance of counting cow–calf pairs. We would work our way up to cow shit-shovelling techniques.

CHAPTER 10

My ALARM RANG AT SIX THIRTY IN THE MORNINGS. By unspoken agreement, my parents would leave me alone while I ate my oatmeal and in return I wouldn't snap, scowl, or bite. At least I no longer had to worry about Mike showing up since Travis had him busy, and I didn't have to make dashes for the bathroom to avoid seeing him when I heard his annoying knock. My parents probably thought oatmeal didn't agree with my stomach. Mike didn't agree with my stomach.

I started my mornings with a head count. Thirty calves, thirty cows, thirty calf–cow pairs. Except one morning, they weren't all huddled near the dugout looking bored with life. I heard an awful bawling and jogged awkwardly in my borrowed rubber boots along the barbwire fence toward the noise. As I neared where the pasture dipped, I could see an agitated group of mamas crowding a calf that had managed to get tangled in the barbwire.

"What were you doing way over here?" I demanded, breathing heavily. I crouched down, bracing myself on the fencepost near the calf. The calf's mama rushed at me. I screeched and fell backward off my haunches. I scrambled back in a crab walk and up onto my feet. The cow stood protectively near her calf as I dusted off my backside. From a safe distance, I assessed the situation. The calf had been stuck for awhile. He had given up struggling against the wire that had worked tight around his neck and front leg. He lay twisted on his side, bawling. This was beyond my mom's tutorial. Well, almost.

"If there's any trouble with the calves, fetch Mike," she had said.

I looked in the direction of the ranch house, which was out of sight from the dip in the pasture. Then I looked across and down the gravel road at the Hayes place. It was closer to run there than to my Jeep. *Please let me find Travis first*, I thought. Anyone but Mike. I had always gotten along well with Travis and his wife, Emily.

The driveway to the Hayes house branched to two bungalow-style houses. The bigger, bluish-grey house on the right was Edith and Peter's. The pretty yellow one with the white veranda on the left, my favourite, was Travis and Emily's. The houses were older and not as well kept as my parents' house, but it was a beautiful property with plenty of flowerbeds and greenery growing freely. I stood at the fork for a moment, looking stupidly from one house to the other. Neither showed signs of anyone home. I hoped everyone wasn't out in the field.

Before I could decide which door to knock on, the front door of the main house opened and out stepped a teenage boy with dark hair and olive-coloured skin. He was too old to be one of Travis and Emily's three kids. Their oldest boy, Levi, would only be twelve years old, making Madison ten and Graham eight. I used to spend hours building puzzles and colouring with them. The teenager didn't look surprised to see a stranger standing in the road. His eyes travelled shamelessly from my head to my toes and not quite all the way back up again.

"Hi," I said, fighting the urge to cross my arms over my chest.

"Hey."

"Is Travis around?"

"He's at the other house. Aunt Emily, too," he said with a smirk. Embarrassed, I stepped toward the smaller house. "That's Uncle Mike's house. I meant the new house." He pointed through the trees and across the field. I could see bits of a house and the framework for a very large barn.

"Oh," I said, surprised. I had once imagined us living in that house one day. "Is Mike home? I'm kind of in a hurry and need someone quick."

"Mike's at the new house, too, but maybe I can be of service," the little pervert said. I glared at him. "Okay, okay. I'm supposed to be helping haul cows. Gramps is pissed off 'cause I slept in, but Grams gave me the keys. Want a ride?"

The girls in his high school probably swooned at his feet. He creeped me out, but I was in a hurry and got into Edith's car with him.

"Who are you, anyway?" I asked.

"Austin."

"Oh, Claire's kid."

The mysterious oldest child, Claire. I only ever knew her from pictures. She lived abroad, that alone making her a super being worthy of worship at the Hayes farm and in the greater part of Kingsley. Laura and her husband farmed a few range roads over.

"Who are you?" he asked.

"Amiah."

"No way!" he exclaimed and slapped the steering wheel. Those British manners people talked about hadn't rubbed off on him.

Austin was still wearing a stupid grin when we arrived at a fancy, if not slightly pretentious, two-storey house. I opted to wait outside on the deck. A couple minutes later, I could hear people in the porch talking as they put on their boots.

"No one told me she was hot," Austin said.

"Stay away from 'hot,'" another voice said. "'Hot' is trouble."

My face was burning. I pretended to be admiring the

construction on the barn yonder when Austin and Travis stepped out on the deck. Travis wore a pair of cowboy boots and a cowboy hat. His beer belly was a little bigger, but otherwise he was same old Travis.

"Been awhile," I said, feeling foolish as soon as the words came out of my mouth. I missed him and his ready smile, but he didn't smile at me.

"Not long enough," he said. "What's the problem?"

"We have a calf stuck in the fence," I said, stubbornly looking him in the face. I had nothing to be ashamed of.

Travis rubbed his face and glanced at Austin, who stood in the doorway smoothing the hair swooping across his forehead. Travis shook his head, obviously thinking Austin as capable of the job as I was.

"Mike!" Travis hollered into the house. "There's a calf hung up at the Williams farm."

"On it, boss. I'll meet you at the shoots," Mike called back. He appeared at the door as he put on his ball cap. "Good morning, Miah."

Austin was grinning again. Travis had already turned his back and started toward the barn. "Austin," he called.

Reluctant to leave us, his source of entertainment, Austin groaned and followed.

As Mike and I climbed into his truck, I told him the calf was caught in the dip. He knew exactly where I meant. He seemed comfortable as we rumbled along the gravel, but I wasn't. My hip hurt from being pressed against the door, the furthest I could be from him, and my stomach hurt from being even that close.

"Did you actually buy a ring?" I blurted. I wasn't feeling as brave as I had when I had stormed into the barn on Friday.

"Yes." He took a shortcut by easing the truck down the ditch. The tools in the box of the truck made a racket as we bumped and jolted toward the agitated herd. Mike cut the ignition and pushed open the door. "Not as fancy as the one in the *Inquirer*, but a ring," he said before hopping out.

The sound of the calf broke my heart.

"Stay away from that one," I said, pointing at the

particularly angry cow. "She tried to kill me."

Mike briefly explained what had to be done and then passed me a rope and wire cutters. My mouth opened but no words came out. I hadn't realized he would actually need my help. Maybe Austin should have come. Mike turned his ball cap backwards and grinned his Coca Cola ad-worthy grin.

"Let's rock and roll," he said.

Mike leaped the barbwire fence. He ran one direction, then quickly changed directions and ran in the other, playing bullfighter. Or would it be cow fighter? The cow followed, temporarily distracted from her calf. I tied one end of the rope around the calf's neck and the other around the nearest fence post. It would have taken someone with steadier and stronger hands a lot less time, but I managed to snip in four places the barbwire that was tangled around the calf. I kept glancing at the rest of the cows. They watched but were indifferent to the process, unlike the mama, who Mike kept hollering at as he darted back and forth like a lunatic. At last the calf struggled to his feet.

"Done," I called, smiling from ear to ear. I did it!

Mike's shirt was drenched with sweat, but he was smiling too once he was on my side of the fence again. The rope was long enough for him to inspect the calf at a safe distance. Some missing patches of hair and some scratches, but no major injuries. Mike injected antibiotics into the calf's neck using a 16-gauge needle, which to me looked more like the tip of a pen than a needle. Then we reunited the cow–calf pair.

"I'm starving. Any banana bread left?" Mike asked. "Don't tell Judith, but yours is better."

CHAPTER 11

A RUSTY VOLKSWAGEN AS OLD AS ME FREED UP A SPOT
in the school parking lot. After I parked my Jeep, Mom and I
joined the stream of people flowing toward Main Street, pulling wagons and carrying blankets, ice boxes, and lawn chairs.
On any other day, parents would have found the kids weaving
in between them irritating, but today it was memory-making.
Everyone in the county came to town in sandals and sunglasses for the Canada Day celebration. Almost everyone.

The sunshine, the break from the farm, and the kids'
enthusiasm put me in a good mood. Coming had been Mom's
idea. Dad was well enough to spend a few hours home alone.
This was everyone's last chance for a semi-normal afternoon
before Dad's second surgery.

Mom got sidetracked, again. This time by Mrs. Smith.
I wasn't really part of the conversation, so when my phone
vibrated in my pocket, I pulled it out to read the text message.

How's Hicksville?

> Not so bad today

Why today?

> Canada Day.
> Town's hopping

Ha! So hot dogs cooked
over an open fire followed by a
Roman candle show?

> What do you want?

A feature. Promised advertisers
high sales. You've slacked big
time this issue and we go to
press tomorrow

> Will get back to you ASAP

I wasn't worried. Today I was researching Kingsley first-hand. My red notebook was in the tote bag over my shoulder, and I was surrounded by potential headlines.

If all else failed, Nathan and I had a file of back-up articles ready for print. Every week we catalogued the material from both the contributions box and the email inbox. Sometimes Nathan hired Journalism students from one of Edmonton's universities to ask questions, but we usually researched using the internet. Community boards for the town and local sports teams, schools, and businesses were surprisingly interesting if you read between the lines. We had started a Kingsley buy and sell site under the name Edmund Pevensie, which gave us access to the Facebook pages of nearly everyone in town and the surrounding area. Only paranoid people used privacy settings, and even then we had our ways. No one questioned the deceiving Edmund Pevensie—or had read C.S. Lewis's *The Lion, the Witch and the Wardrobe* apparently—as long as they had a place to sell baby clothes and purchase winter tires for cheap.

Aside from my own, we also used Mrs. Pumpernickel's Facebook page for research. She was a nonfiction, slightly batty ninety-year-old living in Sunshine Manor. I used to work at Grandma's Kitchen, which was shuffling distance from the manor. I knew her password like anyone else who had ever paid her any attention knew her passwords, underwear colour, and the name of the boy who won her virginity. (**Breaking News: It Wasn't Mr. Pumpernickel**) No one denied Mrs. Pumpernickel's friend request. And since she was known in town for her terrible short-term memory and addiction to Farmville, no one questioned the random Facebook activity. I justified this moral grey area by telling myself that aside from sending friend requests, we never actually pretended to be Mrs. Pumpernickel. We only read her newsfeed and poked around on other people's pages.

I tucked my phone back into my pocket in time to catch the end of Mom's and Mrs. Smith's conversation (**Pensioners Robbed! Another Senior's Money Missing at Sunshine Manor**).

When we finally reached Main Street, Mom and I joined the dozen families sharing the lawn in front of the Town Office. Danika had her hand on an expensive jogging stroller. I was willing to bet that neither Danika nor that stroller had ever been jogging (**Ridiculous Beat-the-Joneses Purchases**).

The first note of the bagpipes pierced the air. The parade was starting. A cop car with flashing red-and-blue lights led two bagpipers ... ten members of the gymnastics club, ranging from ages six to fifteen in matching blue spandex ... two borrowed county floats ... a dozen homemade floats by local businesses and clubs led by one displaying a bright-red first-place ribbon ... some kids on decorated bicycles displaying purple participation ribbons ... two horses pulling a carriage advertising free hayrides after the parade ... lawn tractors scheduled to race that afternoon ... random kids in costumes practicing their Queen wave ....

Nathan wouldn't have known what to make fun of first. Benton was happy, though. He collected the parade candy, and a clown, who was also my former third-grade teacher, handed him a balloon with red maple leaves on it. Today his whole world had turned into a playground filled with music and laughter. I was a little bit glad Nathan wasn't there to trivialize my small-town Canada Day memories. I wasn't nostalgic enough to want to go to the creek that night, though.

"Who is babysitting tonight? Baba?" I asked Danika.

"Heck no. She loves our chunky monkey, but Baba just doesn't have the strength to lift her anymore," Danika said. Water splattered the sidewalk inches in front of us, startling us both and making Danika shriek. "Watch the baby!"

Armed with water guns, Mike and Austin stood smiling on top of the parade's grand finale: a big red fire truck. (**Baby Traumatized by Volunteer Firefighters**). Mike was staring at me. I looked around to see if anyone else noticed. Mom and Danika were too busy fussing over Abigail. RC was helping Benton open a lollipop. Anyone else? If so, would they think of that article in the *Inquirer?* When I looked back, Mike was climbing down the ladder on the back of the moving fire truck. He jumped off the bottom rung, onto the pavement (**Firefighter Calendar Candidates**).

"We need to talk," he said. The day we freed the calf, Mike had seemed disappointed when I didn't take him back to my parents' place for banana bread. Except not disappointed–sad; more disappointed–aggravated. I had opted to walk home. That seemed to be forgotten, though. Something had changed, like he had regained the upper hand. "It's about the *Inquirer*. I got a lead on something interesting."

My stomach dropped. He winked at me, but it had nothing to do with the *Inquirer.* He revealed a water balloon, suddenly turned, and hit RC square in the chest. Laughing and dripping, RC scrambled to his feet intending to do who knows what, but Mike was already climbing back up the ladder to join his cheering comrades.

"Get him, Daddy, get him!" Benton called.

RC threw a toffee from Benton's parade candy, hitting Austin on the side of the head. Mike found this especially funny. I barely mustered a smile.

The parade was over twenty-three minutes after it had begun (**Blink and You'll Miss It**). At the park, a retired blue-grass band played live music. The band wasn't retired, but every member of the band was (**The Show Must Go On! Despite Banjo Player's Arthritis and Fiddle Player's Glaucoma**). Every organization in town was selling something: the 2016 graduating class sold hamburgers; the baseball players sold lemonade; the United Church volunteers sold freshly baked cakes and cookies. Mom and I voted on the chili and pie competitions (**A Race to the Finish: Diabetes vs. Heart Failure**). There was face painting, bouncy houses, party games, a petting zoo, and balloon animals for the kids. And everywhere was a familiar face.

I snapped a lot of pictures with my phone because people rarely contributed pictures for the *Inquirer*. We often used representative, scenic, or blurred-out pictures. We were careful, very careful. I was probably more familiar with the privacy act than most lawyers and cops. Mostly, though, I enjoyed the day with only a small part of me worried about Mike's "lead" and all the things that could go wrong at the fireworks that night.

CHAPTER 12

"WELL, THERE'S SOMETHING YOU DON'T SEE EVERYDAY," Dad said. He was looking out the window from overtop of his reading glasses, which were perched on the end of his nose. Outside, a silver two-door import with tinted windows and green ground lights parked in the driveway. Never in a million years would I have thought either Danika or RC would ever drive a car like that.

"Not in Kingsley," I said. I pressed send on the email I had been writing to Nathan, made sure to close my laptop, and grabbed my coat.

"Have fun, honey. Drive safe," Mom called, completing my time warp back to high school.

As I neared the car, the driver leaned over from the driver's seat and opened the passenger door.

"Danika's Taxi," he called. Like his car, he wasn't what you'd expect to find in Kingsley. His thick hair swept perfectly across his forehead above one eye with the help of hair product, and he wore a grey designer jacket. He was cute in a non-Kingsley sort of way. Thank you, Danika.

"Hi, I'm Amiah," I said.

"Yep, we met when I was four," he said as I buckled my seat belt and he put the car in reverse. He looked over his right shoulder to reverse, and as he did, I got a better look at his face in the dark. He had one of those resting expressions that as a kid made him look pouty; all grown up, he looked pensive. I couldn't believe it. Alek Rooker, Danika's younger brother. Not only did they look nothing alike, but they had been polar opposites in school, too. A grade below us, Alek had been keen on rebelling and Danika on fitting in. Baba had ended up sending Alek to a boarding-type high school in the city. After that I had seen him only in passing on holidays. He had usually holed himself up in his room whenever he was back in Kingsley.

"What's with the taxi service?" I asked.

"Baba and Judith think you need to get out more and I was blackmailed, so here we are going to the shindig at the creek."

"I don't need to get out more. I get out plenty in Vancouver, which is where I live now." Why was I explaining myself to Alek Rooker? "How were you blackmailed?"

"If I didn't run her little errands, Danny said she'd tell Baba I—" He pinched his finger and thumb together in front of his mouth as if smoking a joint.

"Isn't that why you were ..." I trailed off, realizing the question was rude.

"Banished?" he finished for me. "Best thing that ever happened to me."

"Well, don't be pissy with me. This wasn't my doing," I said, not liking being an errand any more than he liked having errands.

"Uncle, what's pissy?" a little voice interrupted.

I spun around to find Benton strapped into a child seat behind me. He covered his face with his hands and peeked at me through his fingers.

"Ben's my wingman," Alek said. Even when he found something funny, he kept a straight face. The corners of his mouth twitched and something about his eyes betrayed his humour, though. "RC has to work tomorrow, so he's checking out with the kids right after the fireworks and before things get too crazy. Wouldn't want Benton picking up on any foul language. Hence Danika's Taxi."

"Uncle," Benton said again, vying for his Uncle Alek's attention, "what's pissy?"

I groaned. I didn't need any more strain between Danika and me.

"Let's listen to our tunes, Buddy," Alek said. He turned on some lyricless dance music that rattled the front speakers. He had the sound moved to the front for his nephew's sake.

The music drowned out the need to talk in a comfortable sort of way. I wished the drive had been longer when we arrived at the abandoned lease near the lazy creek that bordered Kingsley. The lease was hidden from the main road by a treeline and offered a great view for the fireworks that would be launched from the high school football field on the outskirts of town.

Alek drove past the vehicles lined up on either side of the gravel. A half-dozen pickup trucks were backed up to the bonfire in a semi-circle, their lowered tailgates serving as benches. Heads turned to see the glowing-green eyesore as Alek pulled onto the grass only a few car lengths away from the fire and blocked in several vehicles. I was relieved when he cut the ignition along with the green glow that was drawing attention. We could hear the music outside, New Country infused with hip-hop. I liked it. Alek didn't.

Danika appeared as soon as I opened my door.

"Sorry I had to send Alek. There wasn't enough room in RC's truck for everyone," she said as she unbuckled Benton. "Alek is blessing us with his cynical company while his apartment gets fumigated."

"Renovated," Alek corrected.

"So he says. He's driving me nuts, but Benton loves him."

Danika reapplied her lip gloss with the help of the car's side mirror. Lip gloss for an outdoor party by a creek in the dark. I tried to meet Alek's eye to share in this irony, but he was watching the police cruiser pulling down the lease toward us.

"That's just Bobby. He's probably bored on night shift," Danika said. "The farmer doesn't care if we're here as long as we clean up our bottles."

"I know. I used to live here, remember?" I said.

"A lot changes in two years, you know," Danika said.

"Not really," Alek and I said at the same time. Danika shook her head.

"Did you get my drinks?" she asked Alek.

"Yes, Your Highness."

He popped the trunk and held out a case of rum coolers. Danika pulled out one bottle, expecting Alek to keep the rest stored until she needed them. Holding Benton's hand, Danika merged into the crowd. Alek opened and handed me a bottle. I would have preferred a beer but took a long drink of orange-flavoured liquid courage. It didn't taste too bad. He handed me another bottle.

"Can't fly on one wing," I said. Alek raised an eyebrow at me and I could feel my face warm. "Something my dad would say."

An hour later, I was sitting on one of the tailgates close to the fire. I was enjoying myself, making a bit of small talk with old acquaintances but mostly people-watching with Alek. Warm legs weren't worth listening to Finley Brodowski much longer, though. Alek had left with the excuse of fetching more drinks, but he was taking a suspiciously long time. I scanned the crowd for Danika, who had turned avoiding me into an art form.

"Yeah, so I'm at my parents' place for now. Renting my own place would be expensive and a waste of money. Same with school unless you know for sure what you want to take. May as well wait until I know for sure what I want to do, eh? What are you taking again?" Finley asked.

"General studies, but this year I have to choose a major," I said. I wondered if Finley's high school diploma said 'participation' on it like the purple ribbons at the parade.

"You were always real good with kids. Maybe major in them," he said, as a small burp escaped. He was drinking something out of a Mason jar and his breath smelt of apples. He had made a show of waiting for Officer Peterson to leave before he brought the drink out in the open. "Try it," he said, seeing me eye the Mason jar. I shook my head, but he kept holding it in front of my nose. "Try it."

I took the drink so he would quit pestering me. It tasted like apple pie. Alek appeared with another rum cooler as I handed the jar back to Finley. My head was already feeling a bit fuzzy.

"She prefers beer," Mike said. I jumped. Where did he come from? Standing next to him was his sidekick, Austin. Each held a beer.

"These are fine. Thanks, Alek," I said.

"Miah's bitch, I see," Mike said.

Austin laughed. "Good one."

"Hey, Mike, my man!" said Finley, always louder than necessary. Oblivious, at least he managed to break the tension. He stuck his hand out to shake Mike's. The motion put Finley off balance, and he bumped into the tailgate. He looked at himself as if confused by his own instability. He shoved the Mason jar in my direction and took short wide steps in the direction of the bushes like a giant inebriated penguin.

With Alek standing on one side of me and Mike and Austin on the other, I felt like I had borrowed someone else's skin and it didn't fit right. I looked around, noticing how big the party had gotten. There were probably a hundred people there. Conversations were getting louder. There was a lot of laughter elsewhere. I nervously took a drink that tasted like apple pie. Wrong drink. Embarrassed, I put down Finley's Mason jar.

"Be careful. Fin's moonshine is homemade and potent," Mike said. "Give us some privacy, will ya, Rookie? I want to talk to Miah for a minute."

"Haven't you already told enough, Mike Hayes?" I asked, referring to the *Inquirer* headline. No one got the joke, which made things even more awkward. I needed to know what Mike had meant at the parade about having a lead, but I didn't want to be left alone with him, not if he'd been drinking. Failing to pick up on my apprehension or simply not caring, Alek shrugged his shoulders and left. Austin watched him go with a cocky smirk on his face.

"You, too," Mike said to his sidekick. He handed over his truck keys. "Go get more beer."

We were alone in the crowd.

"So?" My nerves weren't feeling up to small talk and pleasantries. Mike took a swig of his beer. "At the parade, you said we needed to talk about the *Inquirer*."

"Hey, you're the one who wanted to talk about the *Inquirer* the other day in the truck," he said. "That article wasn't my fault. The only 'mutual' friend who knew about the ring was RC. That's what I found out: he admitted he told Danika when I bought the damn thing and, typical woman, she either clucked to the paper herself or whoever she told did."

Mike's lead was to the source of the article in the *Inquirer*, not the publisher of the *Inquirer*. Not me. Yet I didn't feel as relieved as I would have thought. Why hadn't Danika told me about the ring?

"You didn't drink all my moonshine, did you?" Finley interrupted.

"No. Here," I said, handing him his moonshine and hopping off the tailgate. "Bathroom break."

CHAPTER 13

"JUST PEE ALREADY," DANIKA WAS SAYING AS I STUMBLED OVER some more rocks and roots. "The fireworks are going to start soon, and I want to get back to RC and the kids." Her face glowed from the light of her phone as she either texted someone she would rather talk to or checked her Facebook page.

I had probably gone further than necessary into the bushes, but the party needed only one moon tonight. I tried to hide myself behind a few poplar trees to be sure, but their trunks were no thicker than my legs.

"How much have you had to drink?" Danika asked in a judging tone.

"A few. Hasn't Alek been feeding them to you, too?"

"No. I saw you talking to Mike. How'd that go?"

"He brought up that article about us in the *Inquirer*." I zipped up my jeans and stepped out from behind the trees. Danika pocketed her phone. "He said that you and RC were the only ones who knew about the engagement ring."

"Seriously? You're worried about who told your little story to the *Inquirer*? It was more embarrassing for Mike than you. And you're blaming me? Believe me, if it was me, there would have been a lot more revealed," Danika said.

"Like what?"

"I can't believe Mike's even talking to you. I would have let you run away and sure as hell wouldn't have spent a year pining after you. I would have gone to the police."

"What are you talking about?"

"Cleaning out his bank account, for one."

"I left with nothing but my last paycheque from Grandma's Kitchen. I took his suitcases to hold my clothes. That's it," I said. Okay, so I had taken the apology gifts he had given me over the years to pawn. *I'm sorry I forgot your birthday, here's an iPod. I'm sorry I got super drunk at buddy's stag and was grinding with the stripper, here's another necklace.* They were mine, though, weren't they? I was too shocked by Danika's anger to be angry. I just wanted my childhood friend to believe me.

"Every couple has their ups and downs, but you didn't deserve Mike," Danika said. "You still don't. Now he's doing your family favours. He stuck around, Miah, not you."

Danika made as dramatic an exit as stomping through twenty feet of brush would allow. I couldn't call after her over the lump in my throat.

No one will ever love you like I do, Mike used to tell me.

Skirting the party, I walked to Alek's car. I planned on waiting there for him to take me home, except when I got to the car, he was already waiting for me. I nearly stepped on him. Alek was sitting on a blanket spread out in the grass, leaning against his back tire.

"Almost showtime," he said, referring to the fireworks. "No mouthpieces over here to torture us, if you want to join me."

He patted the blanket beside him. Misjudging the distance between my backside and the ground in the dark, I sat down with a thump. Alek reached into the inside pocket of his jacket. I expected him to pull out a joint, but it was a pack of gum.

"Some spearmint gum to intensify your moonshine experience?"

"I'm good. Thanks." I lay down, too, more to stop my head from spinning than to get a better view of the sky. I wanted to go home, wrap myself in my quilt, and cry ... or sleep ... or cry myself to sleep. "No one around here cares about anything but a breakup that happened two years ago. All they see is Little Miah Williams or Mike's Girl. Did you know I go to UBC?"

"No. What are you taking?"

"I took general studies for two years and haven't settled on a major yet. Finley thinks I should be a teacher."

"Questionable choice for a guidance counsellor."

"Hey, you and Finley are the only ones who've asked since I've been back in Kingsley. What do you do, then, if you are so put together?"

"Well, I'm pretty sure I'm a graphic designer. At least 'Art and Design' is what's printed on the degree the U of A gave me," he said. "Is that why you left? Secret, uncontrollable urges to get an education degree?"

"Do you have another drink for me if I answer?"

"No, but I'll give you a ride home. Looks like I'm your only friend tonight. Unless you trust Finley behind the wheel," Alek said. He must have seen Danika storm out of the bushes.

"If I didn't know better, I would accuse you of flirting with me," I said.

"I am. Not much else to do in the thriving metropolis of Kingsley, Alberta."

"Gee, thanks."

He laughed. Who knew the ever-serious Alek Rooker laughed? I liked the sound.

"Even our cities are considered small in other countries. You would have to multiply Edmonton or Vancouver by twelve to get New York or London," he said.

"Helping with the census this year?"

"Yeah." Alek craned his neck to look around the car and pretended to do a head count. "Kingsley's population recently experienced a drastic increase of two. Dare I say it has been one hell of an improvement?"

"Cheers to that. Oh, I forgot, I don't have a drink."

The fireworks started. I never understood what the big deal was about fireworks. I never smoked a joint in my life, but turned my head to comment that the show would probably be better high. Alek turned, too. With his free hand, he gently cupped my face. Then he kissed me. His lips were soft and warm. When he started to move away, I pulled him closer by the front of his coat. For a space of time Danika, the party, Kingsley, the *Inquirer,* Mike ... they all disappeared.

The cracking and popping of the fireworks were replaced by clapping, but we didn't notice. What got our attention was a tailgate slamming with a loud *bang!* We shifted apart, suddenly aware that time had passed but unsure how much time, and both looked toward the noise. People made room as Mike and Austin climbed into the truck and slammed the doors. The engine fired up, and the truck pulled away from the fire with more gas than necessary. Onlookers shielded themselves from spit-up dirt clumps, and a couple of people shouted complaints.

Suddenly, Danika appeared in front of us. She reached down and grabbed my arm, pulling me to my feet. Her long manicured fingernails dug painfully into my skin, and I stumbled forward.

"We're leaving," she ordered.

CHAPTER 14

THE SUNLIGHT HURT. I CLOSED MY EYES AGAIN, BUT THE EARTH SPED
up to spite me and my stomach gurgled. My mouth was dry
and tasted of rotten apples. Memories of the previous night
began to unfold in reverse.

I remembered my mom's potentillas and whimpered out
loud. The little yellow flower-speckled bushes flanking the
porch had been watered with orange-flavoured rum and decorated with regurgitated baked spaghetti.

I remembered feeling like a student in the principal's
office, sitting in the back of Alek's car with my hands folded in
my lap. The awkward silence. Thanking Alek for the ride, and
Danika slamming the door closed before he could respond, if
he was even going to.

I remembered the kissing, or at least parts of the kissing. I
whimpered again and pulled the quilt over my face. I remembered the fight with Danika and the conversation with Mike.
I remembered thinking liquid courage had been exactly what
I had needed.

I knew I should talk to Danika, but decided to wait until the next day. Puking on Danika's fancy shoes wasn't going to help the situation. I slowly made my way to the kitchen where Dad was sitting in his wheelchair at the table, sipping black coffee.

"How was the party?"

"Fine." I didn't meet his eye but heard his amused snort. Since they were self-induced, hangovers didn't elicit sympathy from him. I opened the cupboard for a glass, flinching at the scraping glass-on-glass noise as I unstacked one.

"There's Advil next to the sink. Your mom took pity on you and went to check cows," Dad said, adding, "after she cleaned the porch."

I went back to bed.

I made sure to be up earlier than usual the following morning. Oatmeal and coffee were ready by the time Mom pushed Dad's wheelchair into the kitchen. No rips or flannel with checked patterns on either of them. It was Friday, the day of the second surgery.

As with Dad's last appointment, I stayed home to run errands. At least this time I was included in making the plan. I would have gone with Mom for moral support, but during evening chores we had discovered a sick calf that would need to be bottle-fed morning, noon, and night.

After the first feeding, I ventured into town.

I picked up antibiotics for the cows from the vet and a stack of mail at the post office. Next was Kingsley Grocery, which was busier than usual since it was the *Inquirer* release day.

I bought ingredients for banana bread, but also for oatmeal raisin cookies. They had once been my specialty and Dad's favourite. Mike's, too. It didn't take me long to notice the *Inquirer* headline about me this time. I noticed as soon as I reached the counter.

Miah the Man-Eater!

On the front page was a picture of Alek and me with tangled limbs on the blanket at the creek. The picture was grainy and not intentionally of us, which was obvious by the large arm of a cropped-out person on the right-hand side. The picture was zoomed in, and without the headline it would be impossible to identify me. Overlaying the picture were two smaller ones: one of Mike looking ready to kill and one of Danika, taken on a different date. She was wearing a different-coloured shirt, the picture was from a different camera, and there was daylight that couldn't be cropped out of the background. This was not Nathan's best work. He would have been in a hurry to meet the deadline.

I dropped a toonie into the contributions box and paid for my groceries, including the bacon bits that were half price with the coupon from the *Inquirer*. Mr. Wong didn't mention the coincidence that I had already had bacon bits in my basket and they just happened to be on sale. A sale was a sale. Just as Nathan had said, Mr. Wong had no interest in the *Inquirer* or town gossip. I ignored the sideways glances of the dozen other people in the store and left with my cheeks burning.

I didn't bother to call Nathan. This story was too humiliating, and I didn't need a recap of the rules. He was probably waiting by the phone thinking who knows what about me, and I wasn't going to give him the satisfaction. Instead, I crossed the street to the library to face Danika. While I couldn't be certain Danika wasn't behind blabbing certain bits of information to the *Inquirer*, I was certain she wasn't behind the latest article. She wouldn't risk the unflattering pictures and the story's reflection on her. It was only eleven o'clock, but the sign on the library door read *Closed*. A yellow Post-it note in girly handwriting added, *Family emergency. Back soon.*

Was the *Inquirer* the family emergency? Or did the *Inquirer* create a family emergency? I pictured Officer Petersen, a.k.a. Bobby, responding to a domestic disturbance call and neighbours looking on as Danika beat Alek with a rolled-up copy of the *Inquirer*.

KINGSLEY INQUIRER

MIAH THE MAN-EATER!

- MIAH MAKES OUT WITH HER FORMER BF'S YOUNGER BROTHER IN FRONT OF MIKE!

- 'THAT COULD'VE BEEN ME,' FINLEY CLAIMS

SIMPLE IS BETTER

Get the low-down on the annual Kingsley Canada Day celebration

Local Psychic Predicted Oilfield Slowdown

SOCCER MOM BRAWL
Kids watch fight over bad call

$2.00
July 3, 2015

CHAPTER 15

DANIKA HAD LIVED IN THE SAME HOUSE SINCE SHE WAS SIX years old. As though inspired by fairy tales with happily-ever-afters, Danika's grandpa had built with his own hands a haven with cobblestone walks and more gardens than lawn for his grieving wife and two recently orphaned grandchildren. Danika and I used to talk about everything—everything except her parents' car crash. Fifteen years later, Grandpa Leo had suffered a stroke and moved into Sunshine Manor a couple blocks down the road, and RC had proposed and moved in with Danika.

When I pulled up, Danika's white minivan was running in the driveway. I was halfway up the walk when she stepped out the front door. She wasn't happy to see me.

"Your boy toy is on the couch. Handle at your own risk. Who knows what diseases he carries." She hurried past me with her nose and chin pointing skyward.

"I'm guessing you've seen the paper, then?"

"What?" Danika spun around and snatched the *Inquirer* from my hands. She let out a high-pitched screech as soon as she saw the cover. "Ew! This is all I need! Unlike you two, I have to live in this town, you know! I don't have time for this right now, Miah." She threw the paper on the ground.

"What's with you? I—"

"Baba is pestering the kitchen staff at the manor again. She won't get in your boy toy's ridiculous car, so I had to take my lunch break early to sort out the whole mess." Danika hoisted herself into the minivan, slammed the door, and put it in reverse. Then, on second thought, she rolled down her window. "Don't think too highly of yourself either. Alek just wanted to get back at Mike. It's childish. I mean, Mike doesn't even remember Alek. It was seventh grade. He needs to get over it." Danika backed down the driveway and disappeared around the block.

I stood on the walk for a minute, unsure what to do. I had come to have a civilized conversation with her, to apologize, and instead got scolded. And I had just stood there and taken it! I decided she couldn't get rid of me that easily. I picked the *Inquirer* off the ground and let myself into the house.

The flowered wallpaper, crocheted doilies, and yellowing newspapers I remembered from my childhood were gone. Now the décor was modern and stylish like Danika. Red and taupe-coloured walls, laminate flooring, black-framed family photos, and leather furniture. Mother Goose wouldn't have approved of the makeover, and I doubted Baba did either.

Benton was stacking blocks in front of an educational cartoon about potty training while Abby slept in her carrier. Alek was stretched out on the couch with his hands behind his head. Danika's lectures didn't seem to affect him the way they did me. I dropped the *Inquirer* on his chest, wishing it were heavier to make the act more emphatic. Alek opened his eyes, and the corners of his mouth twitched. I gestured toward the paper, so he picked it up and calmly looked over the cover. Then he put it back down on his chest and refolded his hands behind his head.

"Aren't you going to open it?" I asked.

"Doubt the inside is any better."

"What do you mean by that?"

"It's amateurish. There's no grid. They aren't using proper software. Five dollars say they don't know the difference between raster and vector images. The kerning is off in three places on the cover alone."

"Show-off." I realized now wasn't the time to take offence, but I was offended. I flopped down on the other couch. "Is Danika right? Did you use me to get back at Mike?"

"I could ask you the same thing."

"What? No!" I didn't think I did. Did I? "I asked you first."

"You're hot, you're funny, and we were both bored," Alek said. "Ticking Mike off was just a bonus."

"Flattering," I said sarcastically, though strangely it was. "Well, Mike's definitely ticked. And despite the easygoing country boy routine, he isn't someone I like to tick off."

"Did he dunk your head in a toilet, too?"

"Something like that," I said. "I didn't know he bullied you."

Alek turned his head to look at me, his eyebrows furrowed under the hair hanging in his eyes, like he was trying to figure something out about me.

"What difference does any of this make?" he asked. "We're both out of here soon anyway."

"Maybe I'd like to come back one day," I said. "No matter what we joke about, Kingsley is home."

"I guess we're more different than I had thought. You'll just go back to being Little Miah Williams. Better yet, Mike's Girl. Small-town dreams *can* come true."

"No, I won't. Change can happen. You just have to make it happen."

"Some things never change, no matter how hard we stomp our little feet. But for your sake, I hope for an exception." He smiled. "And good luck to anyone in your path."

"What do you mean by that?"

"It's just a hunch."

CHAPTER 16

ALEK MAY HAVE BEEN ABLE TO RESIST READING THE ARTICLE featuring the two of us, but I couldn't. I told him I was waiting for Danika no matter how long it took. He shrugged and closed his eyes, and I opened the *Inquirer.*

KINGSLEY LOVE TRIANGLE
Miah: Girl next door or man-eater?

Miah Williams and younger man Alek Rooker were caught getting hot and heavy by Miah's jealous ex Mike Hayes!

While locals watched the mediocre fireworks display provided by Kingsley's town council in celebration of Canada's 148th birthday, Miah and Alek were making fireworks of their own on the ground mere feet from the party.

Most readers are probably wondering: who the heck is Alek Rooker? The younger brother of Miah's former BFF, Danika Miller! Out of sight, out of mind, but not forgotten, Alek is remembered for his rebellious childhood.

'His skipping class, sneaking out, and partying left his grandparents no choice but to send him to a boarding school,' says an insider.

Another source calls Alek 'the misunderstood artist type.'

Witnesses say Miah had been drinking heavily Saturday night, including several shots of moonshine provided by an unnamed source.

'That could've been me,' former classmate Finley Brodowski told the *Inquirer*. 'But I would never stab my buddy Mike in the back like that.'

After spotting Miah in Alek's arms, Mike made a dramatic exit and Danika, perhaps worried her little brother's heart would suffer the same fate as Mike's, was seen escorting the couple from the party.

Who will earn the affections in this love triangle heating up the summer: small-town bad boy Alek or hometown stud Mike? Or will two broken hearts be left in Miah's dust?

The article in the *Inquirer* had all the dramatic elements of a great story: plot, characters, love, conflict. Like the first article about me, this article consisted of a couple sensationalized facts and a lot of speculation. I would have written it the same way if it were about anyone else in Kingsley. Nathan could have at least given me some warning.

I glanced at the time on my phone. 12:06 p.m. Mom hadn't called yet, so Dad was probably still in surgery. Benton was balancing dinosaurs on and around his uncle. A stegosaurus on his thigh, tyrannosaurus on his stomach, a triceratops on his shoulder. I wondered if Alek had fallen asleep or if he seriously had that much patience. Benton was trying to balance a pterodactyl on Alek's forehead when Danika's minivan pulled into the driveway.

I peeked through the blinds on the bay window as two people got out of the minivan. Despite grey hair the texture of cotton candy and a walking cane, Baba looked as fierce as ever. Her cane added authority, like the weapon on a soldier's hip. Scowling, Baba led the way to the house as Danika followed carrying Minimart grocery bags. When the front door opened, Alek sprang into a sitting position, sending dinosaurs flying in all directions. Benton giggled and clapped his hands. Ruffling his nephew's hair with one hand, Alek grabbed the sketchbook and pencil off the coffee table with the other.

"Baba doesn't understand the creative process. She needs the visual to believe I'm working," Alek said.

We could hear Baba wiping her feet over and over on the rug at the front door.

"They're clean enough, Baba," Danika said. Baba scuffed her feet twice more anyway. Then we could hear her orthopedic shoes squeaking closer on the laminate floor.

"The Sunshine Manor is an awful place," Baba was saying for probably the hundredth time. "I will make a decent supper for Grandpa. They are serving so-called stroganoff again. It is a shame to call that slop stroganoff. I will make him a real stroganoff."

"Sounds delicious," Danika said, probably for the hundredth time. "Will you make enough for everyone?"

"Yes, of course." Baba rounded into the living room.

"Hello, Baba," I said.

"Amiah Williams, where have you been?" she demanded. "I used to see you everyday and then *kaput!*"

"Are you making trouble?" I asked.

"Bah! I never make trouble."

"How is Grandpa Leo?"

"Some days he is intolerable. That is why I keep my room here. It was my house for twenty years and now I get the small bedroom and the whole place is painted like a clown. It's very strange, but we are proud of our Danika."

I followed Baba to the kitchen where her Danika was arranging the contents of the grocery bags on the counter, including a copy of the *Inquirer*. Baba rolled up her sleeves and washed her hands. Then she unwrapped the beef and threw the butcher paper and the *Inquirer* in the garbage without Danika even noticing. Danika was too busy glaring at me.

"I've been meaning to thank you, Miah," Danika said, her tone indicating otherwise. "Benton has acquired an interesting new word."

"Bad language is a sign of a weak mind," Baba said.

"I'm sorry," I said, "about everything the other night."

I wasn't sure what else to say—or what not to say—with Baba in the room. She had taken her post at the counter. Her knife zipped expertly on the cutting board as she sliced the beef for her stroganoff. The thought of Baba's cooking made me hungry.

"You are not going to hurt another person in my life, Miah," Danika said, which sounded suspiciously familiar. Did she get the idea from the *Inquirer,* or did the *Inquirer* get the idea from her? "How do I get myself into these messes?"

"I'm not here to hurt anyone. And what mess did you get into?"

"Mike was the one who asked me to invite you to the creek. He wanted to break some of the awkwardness, to show you ... I don't even know what he wanted to show you, Miah." I was annoyed with the way she kept saying my name at the end of her sentences for emphasis. We all knew who she was lecturing. "I guess we all know what Alek wanted to show you. Do you know how hard it is to juggle the kids, RC, Baba, Grandpa, Alek, Mike, and now you? Of course you don't, Miah."

"Maybe you should spend less time worrying about everyone else," I said. There was a slight falter in the steady *zip zip* on the cutting board, but Baba recovered.

"Whatever. Mike said he was just disgusted that you would embarrass me like this," Danika said. Then, dismissing me, she turned away and changed the subject. "Are you all set, Baba? I have to get back to work."

CHAPTER 17

"There have been some complications," Mom said over the phone. The nurses at the hospital were admitting Dad overnight for observation, and Mom wasn't leaving his side until she could talk to the doctor. She needed to hang up to fill out admittance and insurance forms but promised to call me once she had more information.

I mowed the lawn, weeded the garden, and fed Cutlet. Cutlet was the sick calf. I think it would have been weirder if I didn't name the sick calf I was spending hours bottle feeding. After I showered, I baked banana bread and oatmeal raisin cookies. I was too worried about Dad to be hungry, but I made myself a sandwich and sat at the kitchen table anyway. I hadn't eaten more than a few crackers and a cookie since the baked spaghetti.

The kitchen clock was old and echoed in the big, quiet kitchen. *Tick tock. Tick tock.* I could hear the grandfather clock in the living room ticking almost, but not quite, in time with the kitchen clock. *Tick tick, tock tock. Tick tick, tock tock.* There were other clocks, too. Everything on the farm worked around clocks. The farmer, the cows, the fields. *Tick tock. Tick tock.* Then there was the deadline for the *Inquirer*, deadline for rent, deadline for UBC registration. *Tick tock. Tick tock. Tick tock.* Even louder, my biological clock. *Tick tock.* Women in Hollywood and fast-paced careers were having their firstborns in their thirties. Not in Kingsley. Not where I was raised. If I found 'the one' within the year, we could date for a year, be engaged for a year, be pregnant for almost a year, and then still be behind. I had already invested so much time in one relationship. *Tick tock.* Maybe Mike had changed. The Mike Danika described wasn't the Mike I had left. I was letting myself think dangerous thoughts. Familiar thoughts. *Maybe it was just me.*

I looked at my cell phone again. 8:37. No missed calls. Mom had to have heard from the doctor by now. What if something was wrong? I envisioned her frantic like on the day of Dad's accident, like I had written in the *Inquirer*. I started to dial Mom and Dad's shared cell phone, but changed my mind. What if Mom got in a fiery crash because she tried answering the ancient flip phone while driving home? Suffering from a dozen more what-ifs, I tossed the half-eaten sandwich in the garbage and went to bed.

The air in my room was stifling, so I moved the curtains and opened the window a crack. I fell into a restless sleep before dark. When I woke there was only a dim, unnatural light coming from outside. One of the mystery novels I had borrowed from the library for Dad was laying facedown beside me like a fat paper butterfly. I lay very still with a panicky feeling. It wasn't because of the thriller I was reading or the bad dream I had been having. There was a vehicle in the driveway.

The headlights turned off, leaving me at the mercy of the dark. A soft breeze came through the open window, but it didn't bring the sound of a car door. My mom would have made her way in by now. It wasn't her. Everyone in Kingsley knew about Dad's surgery thanks to the *Inquirer* and the natural way word spreads. How many knew I didn't go to the hospital, too? My Jeep was parked in front of the house. I was home alone. I thought about the unlocked front door and the open window. If I got out of bed, I risked being seen through the window by whoever was out there. Who?

One name came to mind: Mike.

The house phone rang, but I didn't move to answer it. I couldn't move. After five rings, the house was silent again except for those ticking clocks. My cell phone started ringing on the vanity where it was charging. I couldn't reach it without crossing in front of the window. I didn't want Mike to know I was awake. Was he checking to make sure I was at home where I belonged? He had done that before. Because he cared, he had said. Enough time passed that I wondered if I had dreamt the headlights, if maybe it wasn't the sound of a vehicle in the drive that woke me. Then an engine fired up and the headlights lit my room for the amount of time it took for the vehicle to turn around in the driveway. I slid out of bed and peeked out the window to see the fading taillights of a pickup truck.

I pressed the button to light up the screen on my cell phone. Missed call: Mom and Dad Cell. A tear rolled down my cheek. Of course, it was Mom who had called. Mike didn't know my new cell number. No one else in Kingsley knew my new cell number. At almost midnight, no one else would have had a reason to call me. I dialled quickly, hoping Mom would answer. She answered on the third ring. She always fumbled answering her cell because she used it so infrequently.

"Hello?"

"Hi. Sorry, I missed the phone."

"Where are you? You're calling from your cell."

"At home. I was sleeping."

"What's wrong?"

"Nothing."

"I'm your mother. I know when something is wrong."

"Just a little spooked is all. How's Dad?" I asked. Mom had enough to worry about without thinking that someone was lurking about on the property or that her daughter was going crazy.

"They operated again this afternoon, after I talked to you. By the time your dad was out of recovery, my phone had died. I borrowed a charger off one of the nurses. Apparently not many people have chargers that work for our type of phone anymore," she said. "I must have fallen asleep for a bit, too. It's late, so I am going to stay here for the night. The doctor said he will be back first thing in the morning to see how Dad is doing, but he will likely have to stay another couple of days."

"Okay," I said, trying to sound confident. "Well, don't worry about anything around here. I've got it under control."

"Are you sure you're okay?" Mom asked. "Lock the doors, put on the radio for company, and try to get some sleep. I think the city has made you twitchy. Teddy is on the shelf, if you need."

Teddy was a brown bear with a purple vest that I had slept with every night from age three to ten. Okay, twelve. He was perched on the shelf watching with his shiny black eyes and smiling his stitched smile. I took Mom's advice on everything except Teddy. I drew the line at Teddy.

CHAPTER 18

CUTLET WAS GETTING STRONGER. HE AND HIS MAMA SHARED A PEN in the barn. I was leery of her after my run-in with the mama that rushed me in the field, but so far Cutlet's mama left me alone as I bottle fed her calf the electrolyte-infused water. They would be able to rejoin the herd soon.

Cutlet heard all about my worries. I could talk to him in a way I couldn't talk to anyone else in Kingsley. He was easier to talk to than even Nathan, whom I was missing terribly. No offence to Cutlet, but Nathan answered back and wasn't destined to be someone's dinner. But Vancouver seemed a world away, and whenever I had Nathan on the phone, my Kingsley worries seemed foolish and insignificant, so I glossed over them. I was alone.

Dad wasn't recuperating as well as Cutlet. Dad's fever started the day after his surgery and still hadn't gone down. Mom asked me to deliver a list of things to the hospital. Some clothes, slippers, the phone charger, and a book. She didn't want to leave Dad's side. I was grateful for the trip. I wanted to see Dad. Something didn't feel right, and I wanted to be with my parents at the hospital, even if only for the afternoon.

The fuel gauge in my Jeep pointed to empty or I would have waited until the next town to stop for gas. On a hot, summer Sunday, the Kingsley truck stop was especially busy. I waited behind a pack of motorcycles for an available pump and then pumped my own gas because the only attendant was juggling three other vehicles. I swear I could feel people staring at me, getting a better look than the cover of the *Inquirer* provided. I caught one man's eye before he could look away. I recognized him from the vet office. He smiled and nodded hello.

The sign taped to the store's door read *Gas Attendant Wanted*. As I stood on display in line to pay, my eye was drawn to the back of a strawberry-blonde head disappearing around the candy aisle. Tamara Ennis? I hadn't seen or thought of her for a long, long time—particularly considering I had gone what seemed like an eternity thinking about her every hour of every day. What she looked like, sounded like, smelt like. I could pick out her perfume in a department store. My brain had once been a spider web catching facts about Tamara Ennis. New to the Kingsley area. A registered nurse. Jogger. Used to jog by Trenton Auto Body in her spandex shorts and florescent sports bras. Green, pink, blue.

Finley Brodowski joined the line behind me.

"How were you feeling after Wednesday night?" he asked, too loudly.

"Fine." I wasn't in the mood for small talk, especially with him. "Apparently you weren't feeling so well, though, being so full of bullshit. I read what you said in the *Inquirer*."

"Hey now, don't be like that."

I wanted to slap the big grin off his chubby face. He liked that the other people in line were watching us. I paid for my gas and returned to my Jeep without another word to Finley and before Tamara could spot me, if it was even her. The further away from Kingsley I drove, the lighter I felt. By the time I reached the University of Alberta hospital in Edmonton,

I was feeling more optimistic and ready to hear some good news from the doctors.

"Hi, Mom."

Mom was sitting in a leather chair and staring but not seeing out the window. I set her suitcase down beside the bed. Dad was asleep. He looked frail in the hospital bed. The blue and white hospital gown with IV and heart monitor for accessories didn't help.

"Let's go for a walk. I need a coffee," Mom said.

We made our way to the cafeteria where I ordered a bottle of water. My nerves were jittery enough without coffee.

"He's got an infection. It's not responding to treatment. The doctor is talking about amputating his leg." Mom was speaking in a bizarrely detached way. I thought I was going to throw up.

"But why? He can't."

Mom shrugged. "We need to sell the cows sooner than later in any case. This could mean weeks in the hospital, months of recovery, and, well, years without a leg. Your dad and I won't be able to manage them, especially while we are here. And we could use the money. Don't say anything to anyone, though," she said. "Some people are greedy, and if they know we are desperate, it will drive down the price of the herd. As for the amputation, we need to wrap our own heads around it first."

I nodded, unable to speak.

"Hopefully nothing changes Travis's mind about those cows."

Nothing or no one, like his jilted younger brother Mike. Thankfully, Mom wouldn't find the latest issue of the *Inquirer* here.

"Is there any reason anyone would have been out at the farm last night?" I asked.

"No, why?"

"A truck pulled into the driveway when you had called but no one came to the door."

"That was pretty late. What did the truck look like?"

"When I got to the window, it was leaving, and I didn't get

a good look in the dark," I said. I fidgeted with the zipper on my sweater. "I think it was Mike."

"Oh, well, maybe he was checking the sick calf or forgot something in the barn. I had called and told him I'd be gone for a few days. He'll be back and forth between the farms as he helps Travis and sprays the fields."

"That's probably what he'd say," I said, more to myself than to my mom. It was a perfectly logical excuse. His excuses usually were.

"Exactly," Mom said. "So mystery solved. You can sleep easy tonight."

Dad was still sleeping when we got back to his room. Mom put her hand on his forehead, and then flipped her hand over to check his temperature with the other side. An hour later, Dad woke up for about twenty minutes, during which time the nurse came to replace the medication hooked to his IV. The doctor still hadn't come when I had to leave to feed Cutlet.

Back in my old bedroom, I opened a hidden pocket inside my suitcase and pulled out a prescription bottle. My doctor in Vancouver prescribed the medication almost two years ago. I needed the pills only when I had an attack, and I rarely had attacks anymore. I hadn't had one in almost a year. I set the bottle on the nightstand beside my bed and dialled Nathan, feeling like an alcoholic trying to reach her sponsor as she stared down a mickey of vodka. He answered on the second ring.

"Amiah! You're the Angelina to my Brad."

"What are you talking about?"

"One of the most famous pop culture topics of the new millennium, Brangelina. Except combining the names Mike and Miah gives you Miah, and combining Miah and Mike gives you Mike. That's unfortunate, but sales have skyrock-eted. We've never sold so many copies. I'm ordering a reprint. A reprint, Miah!"

I was irritated that Nathan didn't ask me first. Granted, he was editor-in-chief for the *Inquirer,* but these specific articles did involve me on a more personal level than usual. Maybe I should have tried talking to Cutlet instead. Nathan was making me more anxious.

"Who says the extra sales are because of me and not because of the Canada Day piece or Deirdre's advice?" I was particularly proud of Deirdre's advice this issue.

> Dear Deirdre,
> What do I do about my neighbour dog's incessant barking?
> Sleepless on Sparrow Street

> Dear Sleepless,
> After a polite conversation with your neighbour dog's owner, you have two choices: a shotgun or the peace officer.
> Yours truly,
> Deirdre

I even referred to the appropriate bylaw and provided the phone number for the peace officer.

"Yeah, nice try," Nathan said. "Are you okay?"

"I think we may have gone too far." By *we*, I meant him. Mostly.

"How far is too far? Is there something else going on I should know about? Are you sure you're okay?"

I ended up telling him about Dad and the amputation, off the record, which made me feel a little bit better. Once I got off the phone, I changed into my work clothes and pulled on my borrowed rubber boots. I left the pills unopened on the nightstand.

CHAPTER 19

THE NEXT DAY I EXAMINED THE WOLF LIST. I NEEDED TO KEEP busy, to feel like I was doing something constructive. *Fix fence on southeast section.* That's where the calf had gotten tangled up. I remembered seeing the gathered supplies: barbwire, a half-dozen posts, U-shaped nails, a post digger, a hammer. It wasn't like Dad to leave a job half-finished, especially when it concerned the herd. I replaced the rotting posts fairly easily. Pounding in the nails that held the barbwire in place was tricky, but I did it. Then I crossed it off the list.

I was feeling proud of myself until I looked at the list to see what I could do next. *Build grain bins.* I didn't know what a grain bin was, let alone how to build one. I wasn't going to go to the hardware store for advice just to get gawked at either. *Clear tree line*—no. *Service combine and grain truck*—no. *Resurrect old red.* Who or what the heck was old red? *Re-side shop*—no. *Paint fence, barn, dog house, etc.* Now this I could handle. There were two ten-gallon buckets of white paint marked *fence* in the barn.

I decided to start at the front of the property, painting my way to the driveway and then back to the house. The mid-afternoon sun was blazing by the time I had gathered everything I needed, including the cordless house phone and my cell in case Mom called. The dogs followed my Jeep then settled in the shade of one of the tall, skinny Swedish aspens that lined the driveway. Once I finished the part of the split rail fence that ran parallel to the road, I would have a sliver of shade roughly every second post. At least I would return to Vancouver with a nice tan.

Two hours later, I could feel sweat sliding down my back and the house looked like a mirage in the distance. I was considering quitting for the day when the house phone started to ring. I wiped the back of my hand across my sweaty forehead and then noticed the paint on my hands. I tried wiping my hands in the grass, but the grass stuck to my fingers. Touching as little of the black plastic phone as possible, I answered on the third ring.

"Hello?"

"So here's the thing," an unexpected voice said. "I am bored out of my mind and need some real conversation, and you're the closest thing to life out here in the sticks."

"Hi, Alek," I said, foolishly grinning into the phone. "Ever notice how your compliments are barbed with insults?"

"What are you doing?"

"Painting the fence."

"Wow, that actually sounds exciting. I may have to kill myself."

"I can find another brush."

"How about you call me when you're done?" he said. "We've got to be able to find something slightly more entertaining to do than paint the fence this evening. Ever try mutton busting?"

"Don't you mean bull riding?"

"I'm bored, not stupid. What do you say?"

I hesitated. If we were in Vancouver, I would have been showering and planning my outfit by now. With the phone stuck between my shoulder and ear, I picked at the grass stuck to my hands.

"Ouch," he said, breaking the silence.

"I'm sorry. It's just ..."

"The article in the *Babbler*? Okay, how about I give you my digits? 555-0986. Call me if you change your mind. We'll use code names. You're Moonshine, and I'm Cabbie. No one will ever know we talked. The *Babbler* will be none the wiser."

"The *Inquirer*."

"Sure. Them, too."

I laughed. "Okay. I'll call you when I don't have paint in my hair."

"I bet it suits you fine," Alek said. "You were the only girl in Kingsley who could rock the same ponytail every day and still have half the guys in the school drooling over you."

"Goodbye, Alek," I said. I was still smiling after I hung up. His last remark surprised me. I had been Little Miah Williams. The girl with the sandy brown hair, flat chest, and skinny arms. Average looks, average grades, average abilities. Forgettable. Then I had become Mike's Girl. People knew who I was because of who I was dating, which seemed better than being forgettable. And now, it turned out, someone other than Mike had noticed me.

I started to clean up by dumping the paint in my tray back into the ten-gallon bucket and wrapping my brush in plastic. I was absorbed in overdue self-analysis when Mike's truck turned into the driveway and parked beside my Jeep. It was just Mike, me, and the dogs.

Mike sauntered in my direction, chewing on a piece of beef jerky. The dogs left their shade in hopes of him sharing. He tossed the remaining jerky aside, sending the dogs off to fight for it.

"Traitors," I muttered. Wanting to cut this meeting short, I resumed cleaning and bent to pick up Dad's notebook.

"What are you doing with that?"

"It's a list of things Dad wants done around here," I said.

"I know. He made it for me when I started working here last fall."

Mike had failed to mention that fact last week when we were rescuing a calf that had gotten caught up in the fence *he* was supposed to fix! I was about to say something—really, I was—but it was the way he stood: hard-faced with his shoulders back, his feet slightly farther apart than usual.

"Judith called me," he said. "It doesn't sound like Ray is going to be on his feet any time soon."

I wondered how much he knew. I pictured Dad in his hospital bed and remembered Mom's words: *Hopefully nothing changes Travis's mind about the cows.*

"I think you're right. Hopefully the doctor has good news today," I said. *Be agreeable.*

"Mm." He nodded his head a couple times, then looked down the road as if pondering something. "Travis has a lot going on with the three hundred head of cattle he has. Not sure if the timing is right to add more." The word *if* hung in the air.

"Well, he's got your help now," I said. "You were right the other night, too, about Finley's moonshine. It's potent. I felt terrible the next day." *Be flattering.*

"We've all been there. Drank too much, did things we didn't mean or don't quite remember." He was baiting me again. I bent to pick up the phone, the sunscreen, and my empty water bottle. When I stood, Mike reached for my face and I automatically stepped back. "There's paint on your forehead," he said, dropping his hand.

"Oh, sorry." I looked at my hands and chose the cleanest spot I could to rub at my forehead. "I'm a mess."

"The dogs don't seem to mind," he said.

"Nothing a hot shower won't fix," I said. *Be pretty.*

"Then what? Big plans tonight?"

"No, no plans," I said, quickly. "There's plenty of daylight. I may as well put it to good use."

Mike looked at the empty paint tray and the wrapped brush.

"I was just going to check on Cutlet and fill up my water bottle before I moved onto the next section of fence," I lied. *Be useful.*

"Cutlet? I'm assuming that's the calf Judith asked me

about. She wants me to see if it needs meds and can rejoin the herd soon."

I knew the calf was recovering fine without medication but would let Mike be the one to say so. I had talked to my doctor in Vancouver about this role I played. She called it my survival mode.

By the time Mike finished in the barn, I was back painting the fence. When I lay in bed that night, I wondered what it would have been like to spend the evening with Alek instead.

CHAPTER 20

AFTER ANOTHER TWO DAYS OF PAINTING, I WAS A LITTLE OVER halfway to the ranch house. Relishing a five-minute break in the shade of one of the Swedish aspens, I heard the bass of the music before I saw the car. I smiled to myself and hoped I didn't have paint on my face. Alek parked beside my Jeep and unfolded himself from his small car like a handsome rodeo clown. The dogs lifted their heads, too hot to leave the shade for a visitor without food.

"I thought I'd see if you needed help getting that paint out of your hair," Alek said. "Wait, that sounded creepy. I was kidding. On the phone the other day, you said you were going to call once you got the paint out of your hair. You stood me up."

"Sorry." I couldn't think of anything witty to say.

"That's okay. I get it. I was hoping that if I gave a couple-day buffer, I wouldn't come off desperate and you would be finished painting this fence." He propped his sunglasses on top of his head and took in the length of the fence. "That's a lot of fence."

I noticed he came prepared, not looking so citified in plain jeans and a faded t-shirt, and played along. "It wouldn't take as long with two."

"Where's my brush?"

Alek rolled down the windows of his car and turned on his music. Having half the fence left didn't seem as bad with Alek there. He worked on the opposite side as me, so we were painting like a mirror. We talked a bit but then fell into what I hoped was a mutually comfortable silence. I peeked at him through the fence rails. He shook his head like he didn't know how he got suckered into helping, but also like he was glad he did.

"That's quite the conversation piece you drive," I said as I dipped my brush in paint.

"My car symbolizes all that is wrong with the world," he said. He kept his eyes on his brush and made smooth, even strokes as he spoke. "Other people are suffering war, famine, and catastrophic natural disasters while in our society our primary focus is image. We cover up the ugliness within with superficiality like tinted windows and green ground lights, turning a blind eye to the rust and dents, the real issues."

I stopped painting and stared at him, unsure how to respond. He looked at me sideways and burst out laughing.

"Yeah, I'm full of it," he said. "The car cost five hundred dollars and is cheap on fuel. Some buddies chipped in and bought me the neon ground lights as a joke for my birthday last year."

"Probably cost more than the car," I said, my cheeks burning.

He reached between the fence boards and dabbed my nose with his paint brush.

"Hey!" I slid back and held my own brush up in warning.

"That's what you get for making fun of my car," he said.

Our standoff was interrupted by a truck that slowed to a crawl on the gravel road. Mike's truck. His nephew Austin was in the passenger seat. He grinned, looking back and forth between us and his uncle, who was considerably less amused. Alek and I watched as they passed and turned in to the drive-way that led to their houses.

"Whatever attracted you to that guy?" he asked. "Wait. Bulging muscles. Popular. Super-cool pickup truck. Never mind. I guess I always pictured him with a cheerleader or bar star. Not you."

"Mike could be fun. And—" I stopped, buying time as I wiped the paint off my nose with the back of my hand before it dried. My instinct was to defend Mike in order to defend myself, I realized. Alek resumed painting, waiting for me to continue. Or maybe he would have been okay with dropping the subject, but I didn't. "Back then, in high school, I didn't know he picked on you or that he could be the way that he is." I felt foolish for not having seen it, worse for sticking around as long as I did when I finally had seen it. That's what I should have said out loud, but instead I asked, "Is that why you started getting into trouble? Because Mike bullied you?"

"I wouldn't give him that much credit," Alek said. The air between us had changed. "What would I have had to rebel over? An orphaned boy, living with senior citizens, interested in art, with zero interest in farming or sports, in small-town Alberta where being different was a sin?"

"I'm sorry. I—"

"I'm not interested in getting in the middle of whatever it is you and Mike have going on."

"He's just my ex."

"He's ticked and despite the easygoing country boy rou-tine, he isn't someone you like to tick off, remember?" He set his brush on the edge of the paint can. "Maybe it's time for me to clear out anyway. I have a couple deadlines coming up."

Maybe I should write the next article in the Love Triangle series: **Miah Puts Foot in Mouth**.

That night Nathan called. Nathan never called. Scared something else was wrong, I hesitated to answer the phone.

"I ordered the reprint," he said. "It will be delivered tomor-row. Advertisers ate up the chance for discounted ad space."

"I'm done."

"Well, it's about time. Come home."

"That's not what I meant. I can't leave Kingsley. Not with Dad in the hospital. I meant I'm done with the *Inquirer*."

"What do you mean done with the *Inquirer?* What's going on? Are you okay?"

"I'm fine," I said, which wasn't completely true. I had been texting him and talking on the phone with Mom daily, but I had only *really* been talking to Cutlet. My days consisted of doing chores, painting, researching UBC's education program, and avoiding my red notebook. "It's just run its course."

"I don't believe you. You sound like the girl I met two years ago in English 101, the old Miah," he said. Nathan never called me Miah. When he had introduced himself to that shy country misfit, he belted out "That's Amiah!" to the famous melody of "That's Amore." He said my name was too beautiful to shorten. It made me sad to hear him shorten it.

"I've got to go," I said and hung up.

CHAPTER 21

I HAD ANOTHER RESTLESS NIGHT AND WOKE WITH A HEADACHE. After pressing the snooze button four times, I got dressed and skipped breakfast. Instead of checking the cows first like most mornings, I headed straight for the barn to see Cutlet. Not even the smell of the green fields and the warmth of the rising sun eased my inner turmoil. I raised my hand to shove open the broken door in mid-stride, but it didn't budge. A sharp pain shot through my wrist as it jarred against the wood. I clutched my wrist and conjured up a string of profanity that would make a trucker proud. The knob turned from the inside, and the door opened to reveal Mike Hayes.

"I fixed the latch," he said. "You can mark it off the list now."

"What are you doing here? Where's your truck?"

"I parked on the other end of the barn. I have some hay to unload for Cutlet."

I didn't like the condescending way he said *Cutlet*. I didn't like how he always had an excuse. And I really didn't like that he then followed me to where the cow–calf pair was penned.

"You and Rookie sure looked cozy yesterday afternoon. Not as cozy as the night of the fireworks, mind you."

"Alek was bored at Danika's. He was just helping paint the fence," I said. I was a single, twenty-five-year-old woman explaining herself to her ex. How did he make me feel guilty when I had nothing to feel guilty about?

"Ray hired me. If you needed help, you should have asked me."

"He offered." Mike drove by and saw me painting that fence every day. He never once offered to help—not that I wanted him to.

I busied myself preparing Cutlet's bottle. Mike lowered the tailgate of his truck, climbed into the box, and tossed three square bales into the pen. He jumped down and, using the pocket knife he always carried, started cutting the twine that held the bales together. I wished he would hurry and leave.

"Did you hear about that junk on wheels Rookie drives?"

"What are you talking about?"

Mike straightened so he could watch my reaction. "Vandalism."

"What? Why?"

"Wasn't me. I was having a beer with RC and the guys," Mike said with a shrug. "Ask your boyfriend."

"I don't have a boyfriend."

"Well, if he's just a friend, I'm inviting myself on your next girls' night."

"You're one to talk," I muttered. I knew better. Actions had consequences, and with Mike the consequences were always more severe than the actions.

"Are we really going to talk about Tamara Ennis again?"

"I think I saw her at the truck stop the other day. I didn't realize she was still around."

"We had a thing after you left," he said.

The revelation, even two years later and knowing what I knew, felt like a knee to the stomach. "What happened to

'She's not my type,' 'We're just friends,' and 'I don't know why she called my cell at two in the morning'?"

"Maybe all your nagging made me wonder if there was something there."

I had to remind myself to breathe. I didn't know what was true and what wasn't. I only ever had little wisps of information, and if something seemed to solidify and I reached for it, it evaporated before I could hold on. "So you're saying I'm the reason you went out with her?"

"Maybe. You were the reason I broke it off with her, though. I was still hooked on you. I tried telling you that, but you changed your number." He gently took the bottle I had prepared from my hand and set it down. "Maybe I still am hooked on you."

"Don't say that," I said. He closed the distance between us. "Just don't." My voice was too quiet. My uncertainties about what was best for everyone weighted me to the spot. Mike reached for my face with both hands and kissed me. His tongue pushed into my mouth like a slimy break and enter. Something fragile I had been building inside myself the last two years broke. I couldn't do anything but wait for the kiss to be over.

After he had left and I managed to unroot myself from that spot, I fed Cutlet. Then I returned to the house and sat in my childhood bedroom. Nothing had changed. The whole point of leaving and the *Inquirer* was for things to change. I opened the vanity drawer. Among the girlie knickknacks—brush, comb, ponytail holders, ChapStick, mascara, jewellery—was a tube of bright-red lipstick. I had found it in Mike's truck almost six months before I left Kingsley, but I never told anyone, not even Mike. Tamara Ennis was the only girl I knew who wore bright-red lipstick. Mike had hated questions, hated being questioned. No matter how I had asked, he could never quite answer questions about Tamara the same way twice. I had hidden the lipstick in plain sight at my parents' house because I couldn't keep it in our house and yet couldn't bring myself to throw it away. It was proof I hadn't been paranoid.

A horn beeped. I looked out the window to see a Purolator

delivery truck pulling up the driveway. I shut the vanity drawer and went out on the porch to sign for what I expected to be farm supplies.

The driver didn't step out of the truck with his clipboard, though. A smiling, beach-ready passenger hopped out, dropped his duffle bag beside his sandalled feet, and opened his arms wide. "Are we still on the map?"

"Nathan!" Breaking from the trance I had been in since the barn incident, I ran down the steps, across the lawn, and into his arms.

"Now I know for sure I needed to come. You're never this affectionate."

"What are you doing here?" I asked, my arms still wrapped around his neck. "How did you...?"

"I bought a one-way plane ticket to Edmonton. Then for a crisp fifty-dollar bill, my friend Sanjit gave me a ride on the way to deliver the reprint of the *Inquirer*."

"Special delivery," Sanjit called from the driver's seat of the delivery truck. "Now shut the door so I can go."

PREACHER'S DAUGHTER CAUGHT
~~SKINNY~~ DIPPING!

1ST EVER RERINT!!
with additional photos and love triangle reveals inside

...which is worse!

KINGSLEY
INQUIRER

MIAH THE MAN-EATER!

- MIAH MAKES OUT WITH HER FORMER BF'S YOUNGER BROTHER IN FRONT OF MIKE!

- 'THAT COULD'VE BEEN ME,' FINLEY CLAIMS

SIMPLE IS BETTER

Get the low-down on the annual Kingsley Canada Day celebration

Local Psychic Predicted Oilfield Slowdown

SOCCER MOM BRAWL
Kids watch fight over bad call

$2.00
July 3, 2015

CHAPTER 22

NATHAN'S TIMING WAS PERFECT. THE HEAT COULD LAST ONLY SO LONG in Alberta before a thunderstorm. The clouds rolled and darkened overhead, and static filled the air. I couldn't continue painting the fence if it was going to rain. I couldn't survive another night on the farm alone, either.

Nathan looked like an overgrown child with tight blond curls cut short to his head, bright blue eyes, and a cleft chin. We were the same age, but he looked younger than I did. It had nothing to do with his board shorts and Ninja Turtles t-shirt, either. Well, maybe a little. He had a certain energy about him. I, as Dad would have said, looked like life had already chewed me up and spit me out.

This was Nathan's first trip to the prairies. Once he changed out of his sandals and into proper shoes, I gave him a tour, which quickly became a photo shoot. He photographed the red barn, fields as high as my knees, and horses out to pasture. After several hilarious failed attempts, we managed to prop Nathan's phone on a hay bale and beat the timer to pose like the famous colonial painting with the spinster daughter scowling at the farmer holding a pitchfork. I saved the best part of the tour for last.

"It stinks in here," Nathan complained as we passed the equipment in the barn and neared the pens.

"You get used to it," I said. I was in the habit of breathing through my mouth once I passed the grain truck, so I couldn't tell him exactly when he would get used to it.

The mama stood to the side of the pen, watching and chewing. Cutlet was friendlier and struggled to his feet in that awkward way of young animals. I opened the gate, but Nathan hovered outside.

"Feel how soft he is," I said, petting the calf.

Nathan wrinkled his nose and glanced nervously at the twelve-hundred-pound cow. He took one step into the pen, extended an arm like a little kid, and poked the calf. Then he pulled his arm back, relieved the task was over and proud of his bravery.

"Come on! It's not like it's your first petting zoo," I said. "You work at the Pink Rooster."

"Touché."

"Get over here. Quit being a wuss."

Nathan inched closer, hesitating when the mama turned her head to watch him. He carefully set his hand on Cutlet's back. His face lit up.

"My friends are never going to believe this," he said, "Take a picture! Quick, take a picture!"

I had a better idea. I gave Nathan a bottle of electrolyte-infused water and told him to sit on the overturned ten-gallon bucket. Cutlet latched onto the nipple, and I held the phone up to catch it on video.

"You are too cute!" Nathan gushed over the calf.

That was when the mama cow's interest perked. As Nathan continued to coo and feed Cutlet, the mama slowly moved closer. Then, with her thick purple tongue, she licked the back of Nathan's neck like a salt block. Nathan shrieked and jumped to his feet. The bucket tipped with a loud clatter that startled both cow and calf. They scrambled to the back of the pen almost as quickly as Nathan scrambled out the front. I laughed hysterically while catching the whole thing on video.

"We have to post this online," I said.

"Not a chance!"

Nathan, as always, quickly rediscovered his sense of humour, but he refused to go back in the pen. By the time I finished feeding Cutlet, the weather had turned. It was pouring rain, and mud puddles were already a couple inches deep on the driveway. We got drenched running from the barn to the covered porch. After we each had a hot shower, we reconvened in the kitchen dressed in pajamas.

"What do you want to eat?" I asked.

"Whatever smells good over here," he said, lifting the foil covering the banana bread and the oatmeal raisin cookies I had baked. He handed me a cookie. "Eat something. You're looking runway skinny."

We were halfway through the baked goods when the phone rang. Nathan won the race to the landline with its long spiral cord that he had exclaimed was *antique* when he first saw it.

"Hell-o, Williamses's residence," he sang. I giggled, wondering who he was confusing on the other end and how many people in town would hear about the strange voice answering the Williamses's telephone. "I am Nathan. Who is this? ... Judith! May I call you Judith?"

Mom! I tried grabbing the phone, but Nathan dodged me.

"Your daughter has been holding out on me. I didn't know she could bake like this. You're right. The oatmeal raisin ones ... Too late. I will make her work her magic tomorrow afternoon and bring you some ... Perfect! What a relief. Well, you can just come and get the cookies yourself, then."

Midway through his last sentence, I managed to snatch the receiver.

"You're coming home?" I asked before it even reached my ear.

"Hi, Miah. I like this Nathan fellow. Is he single?"

"Forget him. What's going on?"

"Your dad's fever broke. I didn't want to be disrespectful

of Dr. Brown, but we asked for a second opinion about his leg. I mean, it's a leg we're talking about! The new doctor, Dr. Gerard, said we don't have to amputate. If your dad reacts well to the new antibiotics, we could be home as early as Sunday."

"Sunday? That's great, but what if the infection comes back?"

"He will be assigned a homecare nurse who will come by daily to change the bandages and keep an eye on the incisions."

Was there a better way to celebrate the good news and Nathan's visit than with a marathon of *The Andy Griffith Show*? Yes, but not in Kingsley. My parents' viewing selection was both limited and outdated like all the technology in the house. Most of the movies were on VHS because there was "no point replacing something that's not broke." They had a flat-screen TV only because the parts needed to fix their old tube TV had been discontinued. Nathan and I took breaks only to replenish snacks and go to the washroom. When the credits of the fifteenth episode started to roll, Nathan pried his eyes from the screen and gave me a goofy smile.

"What?" I asked suspiciously.

"Let's extend the tour."

"You want to tour Kingsley? Why? It's dark, and everything closed at six o'clock."

"It's like being able to roam the set of your favourite TV show," Nathan said. "I've never been here. I want to see the infamous Kingsley Grocery with my own eyes. Maybe I can even meet some of the characters!"

"You do know this is real life, not *The Andy Griffith Show*, right? Kingsley's not Mayberry."

Nathan batted his eyelashes and pushed out his bottom lip. The pitiful look didn't work on me, but twenty more minutes of nagging did. I found myself driving into Kingsley in my pajamas, hoping we wouldn't run into any "characters." Nathan pressed his nose to the window, taking everything in: the high school, the seed cleaning plant, Main Street. I pointed out Mike's and my old rental house. The little veggie garden I had been so proud of was overgrown with weeds, and broken toys were scattered across the front yard. The tour wouldn't have been complete without showing Nathan Danika's house. We couldn't resist being this close without sneaking a peek at the damage to Alek's car, either.

Danika's yard was well lit with garden lights and a lamp-post. Danika's minivan and RC's truck were parked in front of the garage. No other vehicles were out front. We could see the TV flickering through the blinds of the bay window. Then someone lifted the blinds. All we saw was the silhouette of a man, and I punched the gas. Nathan and I both laughed when we rounded the block, but my laughter was nervous. Was it RC? Was it Alek? Was Mike there? Were they on alert for vandals returning to the scene of the crime?

Alek's car could've been in the garage or parked in the back alley, but I realized what was more likely and couldn't let it go. I drove to Trenton Auto Body. A handful of vehicles were parked along the street, waiting to be serviced. I parked my Jeep among them and turned off the engine. One of the two streetlights overlooking the fenced-in lot was burnt out. Positioned under the burnt-out streetlight, Nathan lifted me onto his shoulders so I could see over the white plastic fence. Alek's car was easy to spot. I gasped.

"What? What do you see?" Nathan whispered. There was no one around, but the quiet street and sneaking around made whispering appropriate.

"Pass me your phone." Sitting on top of Nathan's shoulders, I took a couple pictures. It was tricky because Nathan's legs were getting tired and I had started to teeter. "I can't get a clear shot. We need to move to the right," I said.

Nathan grunted and shuffled right.

Headlights flickered between the buildings. A car was coming.

"Down, down! Car!" I hissed. I slid partway off his shoulders as he crouched. We both tumbled onto the grass and scrambled to duck behind some bushes. My stomach lurched as the streetlights reflected off the decals on the side of the car. We held our breath as the cop car kept its excruciatingly slow pace down the block and around another corner.

"Let me see the pictures already," Nathan said, unable to

handle the suspense any longer. I handed him his phone. "Oh no." At least he had the courtesy not to mention how perfect the pictures would be for the next issue of the *Inquirer*.

The headlights and windshield of Alek's silver import had been smashed. Spray-painted on the side of the car in bright-yellow capital letters was MIAH'S BITCH.

CHAPTER 23

"Who the hell are you?"

My eyes popped open and my heart started hammering in my chest. My bedroom was flooded with light. Curled up to Nathan, I had slept better than I had in weeks. We had overslept, and now Mike stood in the doorway glaring at me and the strange man in my childhood bed.

"Well, good morning," Nathan said in a groggy voice.

Mike threw a bouquet of wildflowers on the floor and stormed out. We could hear him hit the wall in the hallway and slam the front door on his way out of the house. I crawled over Nathan, who was playing with the curly blond hairs on his chest that matched the curly blond hairs on his head. I made it to the window to see Mike kick his truck tire and reef open the driver's door.

"Who was the handsome rooster with the wake-up call?"

"Mike."

"*The* Mike?" Nathan's blue eyes widened. "Dang, he's

one fine-looking country boy."

Mike didn't get into his truck. Instead he slammed the door closed and went stomping back toward the house.

"Oh, he's coming back! Get up, get up!" I shrieked, border-line frantic.

"Why is he coming back? He won't try to fight me, will he?" Nathan was on his feet, spinning in circles in search of something. I was hoping pants since all he had on was a pair of snug boxer shorts. "I'm a lover, not a fighter!"

Mike reappeared at the bedroom door. Nathan and I froze, side by side, half naked.

"You've been playing me for a fool. You're the fool, Miah. I'm sick of your bullshit, and I'm sick of this farm," Mike shouted. "You have until the end of the month to get your shit together or I'm out of here and Travis is out of here. I've been nice up to this point."

I opened my mouth to speak, but nothing came out.

"It's not what it looks like," Nathan said.

"One more word from you and I'll break your neck," Mike said. He stormed out of the room again, leaving behind muddy boot prints and crushed flowers. Nathan and I both stood at the window as Mike's truck spit up gravel in the driveway, but I was almost two years away.

I squeezed Mike's truck keys in my hand so hard the teeth bit into my palm. Part of me wanted him to tell me he loved me. Another part wanted him to give me the clear reason I needed to leave.

"Give me the keys," he said. He was close enough that I could smell the whisky on his breath.

"It's late, and we both have work tomorrow. Stay home with me."

"I said no. Give me the keys."

Mike shoved me hard. I hit the back of my head against the wall. Taking advantage of my shock, Mike grabbed the keys and left. He had never pushed me like that before. I knew he would be back in a few hours, or at least in the morning, depending on where he went tonight. I never really knew where he went. In the morning, he would tell me he loved me like no one else ever could love me and he would make more excuses and promises. But I couldn't make myself believe him anymore.

I started packing. If I didn't leave that night, I might never go. I packed some clothes, toiletries, food, a couple of personal items I couldn't bear to leave behind, and important papers, including my letter of acceptance to attend the University of British Columbia.

"Jealousy isn't a flattering colour on him," Nathan declared.

"You're the one who wanted to meet the characters."

"I tried telling him I am more likely to date him than you."

I knew what Nathan had meant but was still insulted. I needed space to think and Nathan needed to calm his nerves, so I did the morning chores while he did his morning yoga routine. When I got back to the house, the muddy prints leading to my bedroom had been cleaned up and the salvageable wildflowers were in a vase on the kitchen table. The bouquet might have been a sweet gesture—if I hadn't known Mike. Gifts were apologies, usually for things I would suspect but never know. And the only reason the flowers were hand-picked was because Mike was too cheap to pay twenty dollars at the Minimart.

The sky was clear, so I gathered enough painting supplies for two. Nathan mostly suntanned, though. I didn't mind. At least I had an actual person to talk to. Even painting by myself, I would have the fence finished by the time Mom and Dad were back from the hospital.

"I don't know what to do about Mike or Alek or Danika or my parents ..."

"Of course you don't. You're incapable of making a decision."

"I am not. I moved away from here, didn't I?" The scariest thing I had ever done was leave Kingsley.

"Mike made that decision for you. And did you really move? Where is home, Amiah?"

"What do you mean, 'Where is home'?"

"Here, or Vancouver where all your stuff is?"

"Well, what about the *Inquirer*? I make decisions for the *Inquirer*." I wasn't referring to font and grammar choices. I helped decide which topics to print and what the contributors failed to consider. Rule three: acknowledge there's always another side to every story. That was important.

"I don't know if that really counts," he said. "We anonymously put in print what other people are whispering about. We make others make decisions." Nathan must have seen the concern on my face. "It's a good thing, Miah. Don't overthink it. Instead, you should take advantage of it. Mike shouldn't treat you this way. He gets away with it only because you let him."

"I finally picked a major," I said after a minute.

"Really? What is it?"

"Education."

"I can see that. Have you told anyone?"

"Yes," I said. "Finley and Alek."

"Finley? As in the blubberball who told the *Inquirer* you have the hots for him? And Alek, the random guy you hooked up with to get back at Mike?" Nathan asked. "Safe choices. Who cares what they think?"

"They're the only ones who asked."

CHAPTER 24

NATHAN TURNED OVER TO GET SUN ON HIS BACK.

"Who's this?" he asked. I turned to see a white minivan slow down and turn into the driveway. "Mike wouldn't return seeking revenge in a minivan, would he?"

"No. This is a whole different set of characters." I didn't know whether I could handle another of Danika's lectures. She parked on the other side of my Jeep and approached with a covered baby carrier hooked in her right arm and her chin held high. She was obviously on a mission. She hadn't come alone, either. Nathan lifted his sunglasses to get a better look. He looked like a cat that had spotted a particularly tall, dark, and handsome mouse. My own mood lifted at the sight of Alek. He looked more relaxed than his sister. Benton was riding on his shoulders.

"Kingsley knows how to grow 'em," Nathan murmured.

It was strange introducing my new best friend to my former best friend. Together they knew me better than anyone, and yet I didn't think two people could be more different.

"Alek wanted to talk to you," Danika said, once the awkward introductions were through. Alek raised an eyebrow at her. "Well, you did."

"I didn't need the escort, though, Mother," Alek said. Danika rolled her eyes.

"What's up?" I asked.

"Sorry for being a dick the other day," Alek said.

"Apology accepted."

"Cool."

My cheeks felt warm, and I picked at a spot of paint on my t-shirt.

"That was pathetic," Danika snapped. "You two don't do anything in private, do you?"

"Nice burn," Nathan said. Danika's mother-hen façade faltered with a pleased look.

"Now can you reveal to us all the real reason we came?" Alek asked. Danika scowled at him and then turned to me.

"Can we go somewhere where there aren't little ears?" she asked.

She used Benton as an excuse, but I knew she didn't want to talk in front of Alek and Nathan, either. She set the baby carrier down beside Alek, and we walked toward the house. I thought we would sit on the porch in the shade, but Danika stopped walking once we were out of earshot. Maybe that meant it would be a short lecture.

"Why were you driving by my place last night?" she asked.

"I was showing Nathan around town."

"Would've made more sense in the daylight, don't you think?"

"That's what I told him."

"So he's from Vancouver and he came all the way to Kingsley just to see you?"

I was being interrogated, except I couldn't grasp where the questions were leading. "Nathan and I are good friends. Why are you here, Danika?"

"Mike would be furious if he knew I was here, you know."

"Are you talking to me on his behalf again? You're here to check out Nathan after this morning's incident, aren't you?"

"No. I don't know what incident you're talking about," she said. She chewed on her bottom lip and looked like she was regretting her decision to come. "I'm guessing you've heard about Alek's car being vandalized. Did you hear what was written on the side of it?"

"Yeah, I know," I said. I pictured the yellow letters: MIAH'S BITCH. "I'm sorry. I didn't mean to hurt Alek, and I didn't mean to stir trouble with Mike."

"Mike says he had nothing to do with the car."

"I didn't mean to imply he did," I said quickly, but she continued as if I hadn't interrupted.

"I just don't see why anyone else in Kingsley would attack Alek. I can't think of anyone else who would write those particular words, either," Danika said.

I was surprised she was doubting Mike. "Any idea when—"

"I fooled around with Mike," she blurted. "It was a long, long time ago and before I had even met RC. It was after that New Year's Eve party we all went to in Calgary. The one where you threw up under the table and passed out in the hotel bathroom before midnight. It started as a New Year's Eve kiss between friends, but kind of escalated from there. I felt terrible, and it never happened again."

My stomach hurt and my chest felt tight. This wasn't just some girl who had paraded in front of Mike's work in her sports bra. This was Danika, my best friend, we were talking about.

"Don't look so Bambi-like," Danika pleaded. "You were on a break. People know about your breakups, Miah."

"What breakups?" Mike had always been a flirt, but that party had taken place in a time before the suspicions. A time when I had thought we were happy. A time I had looked back on, when things got bad, to convince myself I could be better, Mike and I could be better, if I just worked harder. I was willing myself not to cry. I felt panicky and crossed my arms over my chest as if I could hold myself together. Or maybe I was trying to hide the hole that had been punched through it.

"Mike said you were broken up, that you went to the party together because you already had the tickets. It's not a good excuse for what we did, but ..." Danika trailed off and shrugged. For once, she didn't seem to know what else to say.

"Don't both people in the relationship need to know for it to be considered a breakup? I didn't know!" I raised my voice, which I never did. I didn't care that Nathan and Alek were now staring at us. "Don't you get it, Danika? I didn't know, just like you and everyone else in this town didn't know what it was really like being Mike's Girl."

"Yeah, well, maybe I should have said something back then. But maybe you should have spoken up about some things, too, if that's the case."

We stood there glaring at each other for a few minutes. Finally, Danika started walking back to her kids. I could have gone back to the house, but somehow that would have made it worse. Sitting still would have made it worse. I needed to finish painting the fence.

CHAPTER 25

My parents were home late Sunday afternoon. While Mom hovered, Dad shifted himself from the passenger seat to the wheelchair. Dad was lucky that Nathan was there to help Mom carry him into the house. I struggled with the wheelchair, banging it against every step and dropping it once.

After Dad's last specialist appointment, I had silently prayed never again to see him limp into the house the way he had. Now I would have given anything to see him healthy enough to limp. What if the second doctor was wrong? What if they did need to amputate his leg? What if the infection had spread and it was too late?

In the living room, Mom fussed over fluffing pillows while Nathan praised the farm and the farmer's daughter and the turnaround of Dad's health and at one point I think even the weather. I nudged his arm to stop him.

"Sorry. I babble when I'm nervous."

"Nothing to be nervous about around here," Mom said.

"Amiah talks so highly of you both, and you've been through so much, and ..." That time I hit Nathan's arm to stop him. His rambling was irritating.

"What I've been through is an entire week of hospital food. It's enough to make a man beg the doctor to chop his leg off for something to throw on the barbeque," Dad said. Nathan was finally speechless, and a bit pale. Dad laughed. "I'm kidding. I can't wait for a real meal, though."

"We're having steaks for supper," Mom said.

Nathan joined me for the evening chores, which was wise. Something about my dad and his injuries made Nathan nervous, and who knew what he would have praised if left alone with my him. When we got back to the house, I followed the smell of barbeque and the sound of voices to the kitchen.

"I'm just saying I don't think you have to worry about Nathan and Miah ever being more than just friends. That boy is playing for the other team, if you smell what I've stepped in," Dad was saying. Neither of my parents noticed me step into the doorway.

"What's the problem?" I asked. Mom jumped, her hand pressing to her heart.

"Nothing," she said, quickly. "I was just saying that it is nice having you home, and ... well ... depending on who you end up with, who knows where you will settle."

I noticed the latest issue of the *Inquirer* on the kitchen table. Adult or not, walking in on my parents discussing my love life, especially over a picture of me making out with a guy, was humiliating. They both knew I noticed the tabloid, but none of us mentioned it.

"Is Nathan...? Well, you know," Mom said.

"Hard of hearing? No," I said. Nathan stepped around the corner and gave a little wave.

Mom opened and closed her mouth like a goldfish a couple of times. "Hello, dear," she said at last. Then she busied herself gathering plates and taking them to the dining room. We hadn't eaten in the dining room since I had returned to Kingsley. The formality was for Nathan's sake.

Once we were seated around the table, the *Inquirer* might

as well have had its own chair. Everyone was thinking about the latest article, but no one was willing to be the first to mention it.

"The fence looks great," Dad said. "Paint it yourself?"

"Alek helped," I said, looking up through my lashes to see Mom's reaction. She kept her eyes on the mashed potatoes she was scooping onto her plate. "Nathan watched me work yesterday."

"I can't be working when I'm on vacation," he said with a grin. He took a cob of corn but passed me the platter without choosing a steak.

"How long is this vacation?" Mom asked.

"He got a one-way ticket," I said.

"I don't have any definite plans. I can save money on a flight if I go back with Amiah, depending on when she plans on going home ... uh, back to Vancouver," Nathan said, rambling now that he realized everyone was staring at him. "I can get a plane ticket. So how exciting is it that Amiah finally settled on a major?"

Mom and Dad exchanged a look.

"Which major is that?" Dad asked, choosing to be the one to admit they had never bothered to ask. My parents treated my degree like a temporary infatuation, like a child with a new toy.

"Education," I said.

"That's a great choice," said Mom. "You'll have the same schedule as your own kids one day, with summers off."

It was Nathan's and my turn to exchange a look. Other people would have asked which grade or subjects I wanted to teach.

"Sylvia's daughter took Education at the University of Alberta in Edmonton," Mom continued.

"I've already enrolled at the University of British Columbia for September," I said. "Unless I'm still needed around here."

"Maybe *you* need to be around here," Mom said.

"And settle down with a guy like Mike, right?" I asked.

"I'm not saying Mike, exactly, but—"

"So, Nathan, you don't eat meat," Dad interrupted. "How come?"

"It's not something our team does," said Nathan.

"Really? And is your whole team this sarcastic?"

Nathan laughed. "And I thought country folk were supposed to be simple."

It was Dad's turn to laugh. "Well played."

CHAPTER 26

THE FOLLOWING AFTERNOON, MOM WAS SHOWING NATHAN MY BABY album while Dad napped on the couch. My guard was down when there was a knock on the door.

"Miah, can you get that? It's probably the homecare nurse," Mom said.

I was smiling to myself for no particular reason, but my smile vanished when I opened the front door. Tamara Ennis's bright-red lips weren't smiling either.

"You have got to be kidding," she said.

I had often imagined what I would say or do if I ever came face to face with Tamara Ennis. People claim they know what they would do in such a situation. In most of the scenarios that had played out in my head, she would have had a bloody nose by now. Instead, I held the door open with a dumb, slack-jawed look on my face before asking the obvious.

"Are you the homecare nurse?"

She nodded, looking at me warily. "I didn't know you'd be here."

"My dad is in the living room. You can discuss whatever you need with my mom," I said, pulling myself together.

Nathan and I retreated to my bedroom to work on the *Inquirer* under the pretext of working on homework. I was both relieved and disappointed that my parents didn't question my having homework over the summer. I sat at the vanity, which doubled as a desk. The vanity with Tamara's bright-red lipstick in the drawer. Nathan made himself comfortable on the bed.

My injuries felt raw, like they had happened yesterday instead of two years ago. I wanted to curl up under my quilt and sleep. Confrontations don't sound like they do in the movies, anyway, with perfect prose and punch lines. And telling off Tamara Ennis wouldn't help my dad.

"You okay? We don't have to work on this now," Nathan said.

I shook my head and opened my laptop. We had to prepare the next issue of the *Inquirer*. Nathan opened his laptop, too. In case Mom walked in, we didn't want anything incriminating in plain sight, so we were sticking with screens.

In Vancouver, we met every week to review the storyboard for the upcoming issue. We shared writing the feature articles and sidebars. I took care of the regular columns, like Dear Deirdre and Mark Your Calendar. Nathan was in charge of sorting contributions, advertising, formatting, and printing. We had an efficient system in Vancouver.

We had fallen behind since I returned to Kingsley, though. I insisted on helping sort contributions so that we could get started on the storyboard. They were all in the *Inquirer* email inbox, whether sent directly by email or scanned from the contributions box and then sent by email. Nathan and I had a shared folder on our laptops called THE INQUIRER. Inside was a folder for each issue. JULY 17, JULY 31, AUGUST 14, AUGUST 28, and so on. The time-sensitive contributions were saved in the relevant folder. FILLER was for contributions that were usable but not time sensitive. Ongoing topics had their own folders, like THE TRULA/ROLAND AFFAIR. GARBAGE was for contributions that broke rule one. They didn't have a grain of truth or could potentially land us in court, jail, or early graves. Nothing was ever deleted.

I opened a file, read until I knew which folder to save it in, and then moved on to the next.

> 'Dear Deirdre, Our daughters' feuding is killing my and my bestie's friendship ...' DEIRDRE.
> 'Local spellcaster sells love potions ...' FILLER.
> 'Roland suspected of paying off wife's counsellor ...' THE TRULA/ROLAND AFFAIR.
> 'The mayor of Kingsley is a terrorist ...' GARBAGE.
> 'Upcoming community awareness night ...' AUGUST 14.

There were no clues as to what I would find before I opened each scanned contribution. At least most of the emails had something in the subject field, but Nathan insisted on sorting the emails himself. I thought maybe because the contributions from Kingsley Grocery were only picked up and scanned once per week, so they were a week behind and there would be fewer about the recently published issue starring yours truly. I whimpered when I opened the next file.

"What is it?" Nathan asked. He seemed jumpy.

"'Mike Hayes deserves credit for not letting his breakup with Amiah ruin their parents' thirty-year friendship. Mike is even working at the Williams farm in their hour of need,'" I read. Didn't anyone have anything better to do?

Nathan sighed. "Are you sure you want to go through these? It's my job for a reason. I don't take them personally."

"Because they aren't about you."

"I do know a thing or two about being outed, you know."

He did, obviously. Before we had met, Nathan had told his family he was gay. His sister was three years younger than Nathan. Since she had turned the legal bar age, which was nineteen in British Columbia, she frequented the Pink Rooster "to be supportive" and, I suspected, to score free drinks. Their younger brother, who was entering high school at the time of the announcement and suffered some bullying as a result, still barely spoke to Nathan, which was Nathan's only regret as far as I knew. His parents were somewhere in between supportive and disowning.

"Maybe it's Mike writing these things to make himself look good," Nathan said. It was an interesting thought. Would I recognize Mike's writing? I would recognize his signature, but like ninety percent of the contributions, this one wasn't signed.

We had some regular contributors. Often the handwriting and diction gave them away where an alias didn't. Everything was a clue. The subject, pictures, the paper used. We had received contributions written on letterhead, envelopes, backs of receipts, bar napkins. We usually didn't care who sent the information. The clues helped us research articles we needed to write. For example, a picture with Mr. Smith in the background could lead me to his Facebook page, which could reveal more about the event in the article, and so on. We always kept in mind that someone may be trying to trick us, though. If people wanted to stay anonymous, they could. We knew that firsthand.

I filed the suggestion, and the three after that, in the newest folder: IT'S AMIAH.

"I seriously don't think I can do this anymore," I said.

"Take a break."

"No, I mean any of it."

Nathan was distracted by something on his laptop. I didn't know whether he had heard what I had said. As he read, he frowned in a way that made me nervous.

"What now?" I sat beside him to read off his screen.

From: Concerned Citizen (concernedcitizen@freemail.com)
Sent: July 10, 2015 8:38:21 p.m.
To: Kingsley Inquirer (theinquirer@freemail.com)
Subject: Amiah Williams

Am I right? Maybe now you'll take me seriously. We need to talk. Tuesday, July 14th, the truck stop diner at 1:30 p.m.

I'm assuming, of course, you will still be in town. I suggest
you stay that way if you want to avoid libel charges.

"It was sent after I got here," Nathan said. "I haven't checked
the inbox since I left. I'm sorry, Amiah. I wouldn't have kept
this one from you."

"This one? There are more? This is a threat, Nathan." I
started to wring my hands and my chest felt tighter, like there
was suddenly less air in the room.

"Of course the *Inquirer* gets complaints. We can't expect
to expose people and not get a few complaints. Concerned
Citizen emailed us a month ago and then again two weeks
ago, but I thought it was nothing, like the others."

I now understood why Nathan didn't want me sorting the
contributions.

"How many others?" I asked.

Nathan opened our shared folder on his computer. It
looked exactly like THE INQUIRER folder on my computer,
except he had one extra folder inside: HATERS. When he
opened it, I felt dizzy from the long list of files. He chose one
titled '86. General'.

Whoever you are, you're an immature coward. You need to
grow up and find something better to do than mess in other
people's business.

But Concerned Citizen's email wasn't like that general com-
plaint.

"This is the first that was ever addressed to me by name,
isn't it?"

"Yes, but it's probably a fluke," Nathan said. He was trying to keep me calm, but I could tell he was worried, too.
He started scrolling down the list, looking for specific complaints. "There are ones in here suspecting the mayor and Mr.
Wong and—"

"But this time someone was right. They want to meet
tomorrow," I said.

"I think we shouldn't respond and see what happens."

"They're going to be at the diner tomorrow at one thirty."

"Let me go. I'll have a coffee and see who is lingering at one thirty. I can take pics with my phone and send them to you. It could be a bluff. Maybe they will think they guessed wrong and let it go."

"And if it's not a bluff? They could show up here on the farm."

"We have always been careful. Rule nine: when in doubt, ask a lawyer. We've consulted a lawyer every step of the way. We haven't done anything wrong."

I imagined our friend Sammy's uncle, our consulting lawyer with his fancy suits and abundant confidence. Mom knocked on the door twice and poked her head into the room. I jumped.

"Phone for you, Miah," she said.

CHAPTER 27

MY PULSE CONTINUED TO RACE AS I WALKED TO THE KITCHEN where the receiver rested on the table. Tamara was gone, and my parents were watching TV in the living room. My mind was still on Concerned Citizen's email. Someone knew I was behind the *Inquirer*.

"Hello?"

"Hello, Amiah. This is Officer Robert Petersen of the Kingsley RCMP detachment. How are you this afternoon?"

"Okay," I said. I hadn't known who I was expecting when I answered the phone, but it wasn't the police. "What can I do for you?"

"Alek Rooker's car was vandalized four nights ago while parked on the road outside his sister's house, address 4533–67th Avenue. Were you aware of that?"

"Yes," I said. Of course the cops would contact me. The car had my name spray-painted on the side of it.

"I am investigating this case, and evidence suggests you

may be of assistance. I do need to speak to you on this matter. I won't make you come down to the station just yet," he said. "How about we meet tomorrow afternoon? Say one thirty at the truck stop diner?"

"Sure," I managed to say. He had to have heard the hesitation, however brief. He was a cop after all. I tried to sound normal as we exchanged goodbyes.

As I walked back to my bedroom, Mom called from the living room: "Everything okay?"

"Um, yeah. Just Bobby asking if I knew anything about Alek's car being vandalized the other night. Probably some teenagers in town," I said. I slipped down the hall and into my bedroom before she could ask any more questions. I leaned against the closed door, my breath getting shorter and shorter.

"What's wrong?" Nathan asked, putting down his laptop and getting to his feet.

"That was the cops. The cops!" I massaged my chest, willing my lungs to breathe. "Officer Peterson wants to meet me at the diner tomorrow at one thirty. That can't be a coincidence. It can't be. Those types of coincidences don't happen." I began to hyperventilate. My anxiety pills weren't on my bedside table anymore. I looked on the floor and under the bed in case they had fallen. With hot tears streaming down my face—when did they start?—I opened and closed the vanity drawer that held the tube of lipstick. I hurried to the bathroom to check my bathroom kit, then back to the bedroom to rummage through my suitcase. Nathan knew without asking what I was looking for and looked too.

"Looking for these?" Mom tossed the bottle of pills onto the bed. They rattled as they bounced and landed within my reach. "I've been meaning to talk to you about them but wasn't sure if I should in front of company."

Nathan was trapped between Mom and me. This conversation was happening in front of him whether he liked it or not. He folded and refolded his arms a few times before settling with one arm wrapped around his stomach and the other holding his chin.

"Since when do you have anxiety? You were a happy child under my watch," Mom said. She was frustrated, but I was used to her being frustrated with me. I was frustrated, too.

"I'm sorry I'm not the happy child in the baby albums anymore," I said.

"Oh, don't even," Mom said. "Maybe if you had dealt with whatever needed dealing with, you wouldn't need pills." Trust Mom to reduce a medical problem so easily.

"Just because I don't need surgery and there's no threat of amputation, it doesn't mean I'm not sick." I fumbled with the child lock on the pill bottle. Inhaling sharply, I sounded like a kid with asthma who had just made a cross-country run. The pill bottle wouldn't open.

"Since when, Amiah Jane?" Mom raised her voice. Even Nathan flinched.

"Mike! Okay? Since Mike." Anxiety was just another failure. Remaining invisible would have been better than what I had become. I knew that now.

Nathan gently took the pill bottle from my shaking hands. He opened it and handed me one pill. I put it under my tongue, relieved I would be able to breathe again in a minute, that the hopelessness would ease. I sat on the edge of the bed and put my head in my hands. *Deep breath in through the nose and out through the mouth. Deep breath in through the nose and out through the mouth.*

"Did he hit you?" Mom asked.

I wished he would have. People can see bruises. "No, he didn't hit me."

"Nathan told me what happened the other morning," Mom said.

"You told my mom on me?"

"I told your mom on Mike," Nathan corrected. "Someone had to."

A calm had settled over me, partly because of the medication and partly because I was just very, very tired. I lifted my head and when I spoke, it was in a detached sort of way.

"No, he didn't hit me. He'd yell, but yelling was a lot better than the silent treatment. And sometimes he would kiss me whether I wanted him to or not. Like the other day in the barn, but worse. Have you ever stopped and listened to yourself? I did one day. I started replaying Mike's and my arguments in my head. I was whiny and pathetic, pleading for his attention. I hated myself. I was hanging on to an illusion of what my life should have been. I played the part thinking that if I was perfect, Mike would be nice again, he wouldn't cheat on me again, we could have that rosy life that everyone in Kingsley thought we had."

"Get off your high horse," Mom said. "Not everyone was watching you. They were busy living their own lives. Yes, people talk, and yes, people have their opinions, but it is your life."

"Really? You don't want me to be like precious Danika with the husband, two kids, and white picket fence?"

"Why didn't you say something?" Mom asked, struggling to keep her voice even. She still didn't get it.

"I tried," I said. "When I couldn't get it right with anyone around here, I even tried one of those help lines. The guy was really understanding. So was the guy he referred me to and the woman I was told to call after that. She gave me another number."

"So you ran away. You started playing a different role and following a different script," Mom said.

"You had no voice, Amiah, but you can have one now," Nathan said. We were both thinking of the *Inquirer*.

"And if the consequence is you and Dad lose the buyer for the cows?" I asked.

"Don't use your father and me as an excuse. Place the blame where it should be placed."

"I do blame myself, Mom."

"No, blame Mike," Nathan said. "I knew what she meant, and she's not my mother. Why don't you? No one deserves to be treated the way you've been treated."

Nathan had tears streaming down his face, but I was more surprised by the tears in my mom's eyes. I laid my head on my pillow and curled into a little ball. Eventually Mom walked away. Who knew what Nathan did? I fell asleep.

CHAPTER 28

AT ONE TWENTY-FIVE THE NEXT AFTERNOON, I WALKED INTO THE truck stop diner with its red vinyl chairs, white linoleum, and laminated menus. Nathan was working on an article for the *Inquirer* while he waited in my Jeep parked on the far side of the lot. The lunch rush was over. A couple of men dressed in greasy work clothes sat at the counter. A teenaged waitress filled their coffee mugs. Officer Robert Petersen sat at a corner table where he had a view of the entire restaurant, including the door. He was wearing his uniform, complete with a holstered gun. He nodded in my direction when I entered.

I sat down across from him, not liking having my back to the door. It was strategic on his part, I realized. He had my full attention. The only thing over his shoulder for me to look at was a dried blob of ketchup on the white wall.

"Can I get you anything?" the waitress asked.

"Water, please," I said, forcing a polite smile. Bobby

sipped his coffee and didn't say anything until after the wait-ress delivered my water.

"So are we going to pretend here or are we going to skip that part?" he asked.

"What do you mean?" Nathan and I had agreed on a strat-egy: deny, deny, deny.

Bobby sighed. "You know, I didn't care about the little tabloid that first appeared in January with its trivial calendar and tidbits of gossip. A lot of people have been up in arms about the *Inquirer*, though."

My back stiffened and I tried to sneak a look over my shoulder, fearful the waitress had overheard him. She had nothing better to do than eavesdrop on her customers on a slow afternoon. I knew because up until recently I had been a waitress.

"We've received numerous calls at the station on the sub-ject," Bobby continued. "Then it got personal. 'Desperate police wife barters "no tickets" in exchange for friendship.' Do you remember that headline? Released June 5, 2015. I know you live in Vancouver now, but you do have family and maybe a few friends left here who may have brought it up, right?"

That particular issue was released before I had even arrived in Kingsley. He pulled a folded piece of paper from his pocket. A page from the *Inquirer*. He slowly unfolded it, placed it on the table, and slid it in my direction.

FRIENDS DON'T TICKET FRIENDS

Lonely Joanna Petersen was overheard at a local fundraiser bartering 'no traffic tickets' from RCMP hubby in exchange for 'a real friend.' After her youngest of three kids moved out and the tragic loss of her mother, Joanna is suffering something inevitable for most stay-at-home moms: Empty Nest Syndrome.

'A mother's life revolves around her family. Then comes a time her family doesn't need her on a day-to-day basis anymore,' says family psychology expert Hilary Philips, who hasn't met with Joanna. 'The children are gone, the husband still has work, and the woman is left in an identity crisis.'

Insiders say Joanna's grieving father, former *Gazette* writer Jack Whitby, is the closest Joanna has to a real friend in Kingsley.

'There's been too much sadness and loss lately,' Officer Robert Petersen allegedly says.

But what does Kingsley have to offer middle-aged women other than quilting and yoga classes at the senior centre? At least class-goers won't have to worry about double parking anymore!

"Ever hear the phrase *Happy wife, happy life?*" Bobby asked. I nodded. "Well, my wife wasn't happy with this particular issue of the *Inquirer*. That's when I sent my first email as a concerned citizen, not a police officer. I trust you know the difference."

"I thought you wanted to discuss Alek's car," I said, realizing he could probably get into trouble discussing personal grievances while on duty.

"We are getting to that," Bobby said. He took the article back and tucked it into his pocket. I felt warm in my capris and t-shirt and thought he must have been sweltering in full uniform.

"The *Inquirer* walks a thin line. Libel charges would be difficult, but not impossible. This article, for instance, has the potential to cause problems for me at work. The publisher has been very careful, but I can see why he or *she* would want to stay anonymous. I was curious about the publisher, so started doing a bit of research—on my own time, of course."

Next, Bobby pulled out a pocket-sized coil-bound notebook and flipped until he found the page he was looking for. I heard the chimes above the restaurant door sound. New customers entered. Chairs scraped the linoleum as they were pulled out, and the waitress asked if anyone needed menus. It was discomfiting not being able to see them, but I didn't turn around. I didn't want to seem guilty.

"Let's see," Bobby said. "Purolator employee Sanjit Sharma delivers the *Inquirer* to Kingsley Grocery every second Friday at approximately seven a.m. Interestingly, there are no order numbers or invoices to track. Sharma pays cash for the tabloids personally from the print shop near his work and then delivers them off the record while making his regular Purolator drops in the area. He also picks up the contents of the contributions box weekly, scans the contributions and emails them to theinquirer@freemail.com, and deposits the revenue into a company account." Bobby looked up at me. I felt sick and he knew it. "Much of the content for the paper I imagine is from social media, word of mouth, websites, and of course contributions, but sometimes the *Inquirer* hires journalism students from nearby universities to conduct interviews and take pictures. Like small-town paparazzi. Quite clever, I admit. Again—and not without difficulty because I had to catch one of these students in the act—that led to the anonymous email address.

"Then I thought: how were these students and Sharma paid? Sharma could take his fees from the profits in the contribution box before depositing the rest into a company bank account. With the proper paperwork, I suspect the account number would lead me to you and/or a young man fitting the description of the houseguest staying at your parents' farm. Sharma can't legally deliver people. It would be a shame to get fired if his boss found out he had ever done such a thing, especially since he has five kids under the age of ten all depending on his steady paycheque.

"The student I got in touch with, however, received payment via post. Unlike professionals, students are willing to work for cheap and can be paid in cash, leaving no digital trail. The envelope didn't have a return address obviously, but—" He pulled out the empty envelope and pointed to the postal cancellation. "Mailed from a Vancouver, British Columbia, postal code. Who lives in BC and has an axe to grind against little ol' Kingsley, Alberta? I have to admit you threw me off with these articles about yourself. Are we done playing now?"

I nodded.

"At first, I thought the *Inquirer* simply needed to disappear. A retraction would only make matters worse for my wife and, correspondingly, me. I'm not interested in swaying public opinion or getting into a debate about freedom of speech, either. But then I realized I shouldn't be so hasty and throw away what could be a valuable tool. Remember your articles about the baby Jesus being stolen from the church nativity scene?"

Of course I did. Denying it was pointless.

Bobby flipped a couple pages in his notebook and read the headlines anyway. "January 9th Issue: 'Baby Jesus On Ransom.' January 23rd Issue: 'Teenager Suspected of Robbing Holy Cradle.' February 6th Issue: 'Baby Jesus Home Safe and Sound.' June 19th Issue: 'Nativity Scene Thief Strikes Again!!! Garden Gnomes Missing Across Town.' Well, I don't know what's happening with those garden gnomes, but baby Jesus likely turned up because the *Inquirer* sensationalized the crime and freaked out whoever stole him."

"Do you expect someone to show up and repaint Alek's car?"

"No," Bobby said, ignoring my sarcasm. "It'll be like those crime watcher shows on TV. Media stirs information. Appeal to the town's sense of responsibility. You'd be surprised at the loyalty *some* people have to their hometown. The pictures I saw you and your friend taking at the auto shop the other night will accompany the article perfectly."

"Okay," I said, trying to hide my surprise again. "And then what?"

"Then we have another talk." Bobby stood up while tucking his notebook and the envelope into his pocket with the article. He put three dollars and fifty cents in change on the table and walked away.

CHAPTER 29

I TOOK A SIP OF MY WATER, NOT WANTING TO WALK OUT OF THE diner with Officer Petersen. I heard him exchange greetings with a couple of familiar voices. Once Bobby left the diner, I turned to find Edith and Peter Hayes sitting at the table nearest the door along with their pervert grandson, Austin. There was no other way out. I pasted a polite smile onto my face and approached their table.

"Hello."

"Hi, dear," said Edith. "How's your dad doing?"

"Still sleeping a lot, but glad to be home," I said. "How have you been?" I realized how stupid the question was as soon as it escaped my mouth. You asked someone you haven't seen for a couple days, a week, or even a month or two how they have been. Not people you hadn't seen for two years, especially when the last time you had seen them was the day before you ran out on their son. I remembered Travis's reaction to seeing me again and wondered if Peter and Edith hated me, too. It made me sad, especially to think of Travis's wife, Emily. She had been one of my few friends toward the end of my time in Kingsley. I had closed almost everyone else out.

"Oh, I can't complain," said Edith.

"I sure can," said Peter. "I'm paying for lunch and Austin eats like a horse."

"Have coffee with cops often?" Austin asked.

"Have some respect, boy," said Peter at almost the same time as Edith said: "It's none of our business."

"It's okay. Bobby was just asking about Alek Rooker's car. He's talking to a few people in town," I fibbed. I realized they all probably saw the latest *Inquirer* featuring me making out with Alek. I felt my face grow hot and began fidgeting with the hem of my shirt. Luckily, the waitress interrupted with plates overflowing with hamburgers and fries.

I took the opportunity to excuse myself. I simply wanted to go home, but as I neared my Jeep, I saw that Nathan was not alone. Danika stood at the passenger-side window. They were chatting and laughing like they were the ones who were old friends. The only thing I had foreseen them having in common was me. But I realized that there had to be at least a few more similarities for me to have been best friends with each of them.

"Hi," Danika said, surprisingly chipper. Our vehicles were parked side by side, and I could see a video playing through the tinted windows of her minivan.

"The puke machines are in the van," Nathan said. Danika giggled. I wouldn't have expected her to find a joke about her kids funny. Then again, as much as I wanted to make sense of people, I was realizing I couldn't fit people into neat little boxes.

"Nathan said you were here to talk to Bobby about Alek's car," Danika said. I shot Nathan a look that demanded to know how much he told her. He gave me a slight shake of his head, indicating not what I feared. Nothing about the *Inquirer.* "No, no," Danika said, misreading the exchange. "Don't be mad at him. I want to thank you."

"I don't think I'm going to be any help. Bobby just wanted

to talk to me because of the message painted on the side the car."

"Still. You didn't have to," Danika said. I felt guilty because I actually did have to. "RC insists that he is Mike's alibi for that night."

"Mike told me the same thing," I said.

"That doesn't mean he had nothing to do with it, though," Danika said. "Mike does have a temper."

"The truth tends to come out," Nathan said.

"Sometimes it just needs a little help," Danika agreed. If I didn't know better, I would have thought they had eaves-dropped on my conversation with Officer Petersen.

When I pulled my Jeep into my parents' driveway, I spot-ted Mike's truck peeking out from behind the barn. It wasn't in its usual spot but near Cutlet's pen again. Something was wrong.

Nathan followed my eyes to the truck. "Not this character again. Let's skip the drama and go into the house," he said, but I didn't listen.

I hopped out of my Jeep as soon as it was parked and jogged toward the barn. As Mike's truck came into full view, he appeared, struggling with something large and awkward wrapped in an old blue tarp. Whatever it was, it was heavy, even for Mike. He didn't seem surprised to see me. He just looked at me, his jaw set and his eyes cold. Then he hoisted the load onto the back of his truck with the help of his knee. It landed with a thud.

"What are you doing?"

Mike pushed the bundle so it slid past the tailgate. A hoof flopped free of the tarp, confirming my fear. I glanced back at Nathan, the vegetarian. He was hovering about twenty feet behind me, his hand covering his mouth. Of course he would stay a safe distance away after Mike had threatened him. It was easy to say stand up to a bully, but harder to do the actual standing up. Mike slammed the tailgate closed, just as he did the night of the fireworks.

"I'm working, Miah," he said. "I don't get to read books and sip coffee all day."

I had hated when Mike would tease me in front of his friends about my luxurious life. They had thought he had been playing, or maybe they hadn't spoken up because they didn't want to get in the middle of it. *Miah is spoiled. Miah doesn't know what real work is. Miah's parents set high standards for our princess.* I had been Mike's maid, secretary, and worse, and I had still worked at Grandma's Kitchen to help make ends meet. Anger welled up inside me, and if it wasn't for the image of that hoof burning in my mind, I would have told him I would be shocked if he could even read a book.

"What did you do? Cutlet was fine this morning! I just fed him this morning!"

"*He* was not a pet," Mike yelled. "He was a sick calf that was costing the farm money. I did what had to be done."

"It didn't have to be done! We both know it."

"Prove it," Mike said. He climbed into the truck and started the engine. Cutlet was gone.

CHAPTER 30

DANIKA'S EMAIL WAS EASY TO IDENTIFY. IT WAS FROM HER PERSONAL email account, and it was signed.

> From: Danika Miller (danika2131@freemail.com)
> Sent: July 15, 2015 11:42:56 a.m.
> To: Kingsley Inquirer (theinquirer@freemail.com)
> Subject: Alek's Car
>
> Dear Inquirer,
>
> I try not to get wrapped up in gossip and have only ever written to Dear Deirdre before, but there's a time to be quiet and a time to speak up.
>
> My brother and I proudly grew up in Kingsley. Our childhood consisted of riding our pedal bikes to the park, swimming in a dugout instead of a concrete building, climbing

trees and hay bales instead of manufactured playgrounds, and having campfires at night under the stars in the middle of the week.

Even now, going uptown to pick up the mail and a gallon of milk means visiting friends at each stop. I was proud to help with the fundraiser social and to see the community come together to raise money for Gladys. Small-town living is a treasure we have to protect.

My brother's car was vandalized while parked outside my house on the night of Thursday, July 9th. I have felt unsafe and shaken ever since. If we sit idle and let this happen, what next? Breaking and entering? Graffiti on Main Street? My baba says that many wars were started with a powerfully worded letter, and many wars have ended with one as well. If anybody knows anything, now is the time to speak up to protect the Kingsley we all know and love.

Sincerely,
Danika Miller

I read it through once quickly. Then I read it more slowly in order to dissect it. It was written after she had said I was brave for talking to Bobby about Alek's car. She said she didn't gossip and that Alek was proud of growing up in Kingsley. Not quite. She also said there's a time to be quiet and a time to speak up. She had a point there. All the things she had described about her childhood were a cherished part of my childhood, too. I imagined her writing at the desk in the library, risking the image and social circles she prided herself on. Danika signed her letter. Danika was the brave one. I saved the letter in the newest folder: JUSTICE FOR ALEK. I also saved a copy on my desktop.

SERENA IS PREGNANT ... WITH TWINS!

KINGSLEY
INQUIRER

SHOCKING PHOTOS INSIDE

STRAWBERRY RHUBARB RECIPES TO DIE FOR!

VANDALIZED!
ALEK'S CAR SPRAY PAINTED IN THE NIGHT

How Carl lost 55 lbs in 2-1/2 months!

Drunk hairdresser dyes hair and massacres bob

Cook at Sunshine Manor Takes Stress Leave

$2.00
July 17, 2015

INQUIRER

VANDALIZED!

ALEK'S CAR

SPRAYPAINTED

IN THE NIGHT

CHAPTER 31

NATHAN WAS AS HELPFUL BAKING COOKIES AS HE HAD BEEN PAINTING the fence. He sat with his feet up while I did the work.

"There's not going to be any cookies unless you quit eating the dough," I said.

"Make more dough," he said with a grin. He popped another pinch of peanut butter cookie dough into his mouth. Two dozen chocolate chip cookies were cooling on the counter, and the first dozen peanut butter cookies were in the oven. I was mixing together the ingredients for oatmeal raisin cookies. My plan was to stock the freezer before I left for Vancouver. Somehow it made me feel better about leaving.

"I can't make more cookie dough. I'm out of eggs," I said. "You know, those oval things that are supposed to hatch into cute little baby chicks but *you* eat them instead."

"I'm allowed to eat eggs. I'm a vegetarian, not a vegan."

"What's the difference if you murder a baby chick or a cow?" I asked, but we let the conversation trail off because it reminded us of Cutlet. I wasn't a vegetarian, and of course I had known Cutlet's ultimate fate. That wasn't the point.

I moved all of the cookie dough out of Nathan's reach. I should have reminded Mom to buy more eggs when she had gone to Kingsley Grocery. It was *that* Friday again, the *Inquirer*'s release day. The tabloid held no surprises for me this time. On the cover was a picture of Alek's car, except Nathan had blurred the spray-painted words on the side to make the headline more enticing.

Vandalized! Alek's Car Spray-Painted in the Night

The pictures inside the tabloid revealed the spray-painted message: MIAH'S BITCH. Nathan had put a *Censored* banner at an angle over the middle of the second word, so that only the B and H were visible. It was still obvious what it read, though. I had written the article. We had both worked really hard the last few days. I really wanted to help Officer Petersen, and Nathan was obsessed with pleasing advertisers.

MAKE-OUT SESSION WITH MIAH MEANS DISASTER FOR ALEK

Alek Rooker's car was vandalized while parked outside his sister's house in what's supposed to be a safe and quiet Kingsley neighbourhood.

Police aren't revealing suspects but say they aren't ruling out the possible role of the summer love triangle between Mike, Miah, and Alek. Obviously! Along with a smashed windshield and broken headlights, a profane reference to Miah is spray-painted on the side of the car!

'Not only is Mike furious over Alek and Miah hooking up on Canada Day,' a source tells the *Inquirer,* 'but he has spotted Alek moving in on his job at the Williams farm, too.'

This draws question to Mike's motivations and continued work at the Williams farm while Ray is in and out of hospital after his catastrophic fall at Kingsley Grocery.

Was the graffiti the result of another of Mike's angry outbursts, was Mike framed, or is it possible that the crime is completely unrelated? No matter the culprit, Kingsley citizens say they will not condone crime on their streets.

A local RCMP officer warns: 'If not dealt with properly, crimes like these can escalate.'

"'Disaster for Alek.' I'm worried what the headline will do for your love life," Nathan said.

"Shut it," I said, holding a mixing bowl and stirring raisins into the batter with more vigour than any cookie recipe called for. I was nervous enough without thinking about my love life. Of course I suspected Mike was involved somehow and wanted to call him out in big, bold letters like the big, bold letters defaming me on Alek's car, but I also had Officer Peterson and the sale of Dad's cows to consider.

"You do realize you're mad at yourself, right? You wrote the article."

I scowled at him.

"Come on, Amiah," he said. "This is a good thing. We're being let off easy."

"For now," I said. "And technically *you* are being let off completely so far." I felt uncomfortable with the open-ended way Bobby and I had left our conversation at the diner on Tuesday. Again, it had been strategic on his part. He maintained the power. He had me do what he wanted me to do in exchange for a bit of time. Time Nathan wanted, but I didn't. The uncertainty wasn't exciting for me; it was torture. What would happen if we couldn't reveal who vandalized Alek's car? And even if we did, what then?

"The cop even said we aren't doing anything wrong. If he was going to expose you, he would have already. And we would have run the vandalized car story in the *Inquirer* anyway," Nathan prattled on. Teaming up with a cop thickened the plot in his twisted reality show. This time he even had a minor part in the cast. It wasn't that he didn't care. He was just wired differently than me.

"It smells so good in here," Tamara's sugary voice carried from the living room.

"'It smells so good in here'," Nathan mimicked. He batted his eyelashes and twirled imaginary hair above his shoulder. It was childish, but he made me laugh and eased the tension I felt whenever the homecare nurse was around. Tamara talked to my dad like he was five years old instead of fifty-eight. It irritated me.

We had gone to town for groceries in hope of missing Tamara's visit, but she had run late that morning ... again. She had been late three times in less than a week.

"Mom had better not offer her any of my cookies," I whispered. Tamara and I had shared quite enough already. According to Nathan, who had talked to Danika, who had talked to Tamara and been around when Mike and Tamara started openly dating, Tamara had been a rebound and knew it. Danika "kinda felt sorry" for her. Knowing Mike's quiet control firsthand, I would have felt sorry for Tamara, too, except they had hooked up while he was still living with me. What did she expect? Prince Charming?

"Kingsley is seriously lacking for night life," Nathan said. "Maybe if there was something to do, people wouldn't have to entertain themselves by smashing car windows."

"Yes, because that's why it happened."

"Aren't there any barn dances or hoedowns we can go to this weekend?"

I laughed. "Your depiction of small-town living is warped. And even if there were a party to go to, I don't want to go."

"We need to get out, Amiah," he said. "We're going to go crazy. Small towns can be like black holes. They suck you in and never let you go."

"How is that any different from the city? I mean aside from no night clubs, no shopping malls, no fast food restaurants ..."

"Starbucks. For the love of God, I need a Starbucks. And it's different because in the city you can change social circles. Here you are either in or out," he said.

"Getting homesick, are you?"

"Maybe a bit. It's so quiet around here," he said. Tamara's fake giggle carried from the living room again. "Well, usually. You know I'm here for you, but I think two weeks is all I can get away with for bereavement leave for my fake sick grandma. If you're ready, too, at least I would be company for the drive back."

I didn't answer as I rolled the last ball of cookie dough and placed it on the cookie sheet. I felt torn between Kingsley and Vancouver.

"Think about it," Nathan said. "But before I do have to go, I need to diversify my Alberta experience. Let's go to Edmonton tomorrow night."

Getting out for a night sounded fun. I felt guilty, though, like I needed to ask someone for permission and shouldn't crave the anonymity of the city for even one night. I put the new batch of cookies into the oven and started zipping the ones that had cooled into freezer bags.

"Phew," Mom said as she entered the kitchen. "I'm glad I never have to hear Tamara Ennis's voice again."

"I thought Dad needed homecare for a month."

"He does, but the clinic is sending someone new next week," she said.

The county had a health care clinic that managed all of the surrounding communities. Tamara had likely been assigned my dad's case because she lived closest to the patient.

"Really? Why?" I asked, struggling between relief and guilt for the relief. That was my anxiety. Always feeling guilty whether it made sense or not.

Mom raised an eyebrow at me and then set to getting Dad some cookies and milk. She knew about Tamara and Mike. I looked at Nathan, who smiled with that big mouth.

CHAPTER 32

CUTLET'S MAMA REJOINED THE HERD. I WONDERED WHETHER SHE missed Cutlet, and whether she cared that she was the only mama without a calf. I felt sorry for her. I finally brought myself to clean out their pen in the barn. I don't know where Mike had shot Cutlet, but he didn't shoot him there. Mike would have been deaf if he had fired a shotgun in the barn, and there was no blood anywhere. My morning routine was the same as it had been before Cutlet had gotten sick, but it didn't offer the same peace as it had before. Chores were tainted by thoughts of Mike. Tainted like everything else in Kingsley.

When I got back to the house, Nathan was still asleep in the spare bedroom. I had expected to find Dad in his sick bed, also known as the couch. He would be sleeping or flicking through the channels on TV while Mom took up her knitting or fussed over the house. Instead, Dad was sitting up with his leg propped on a cushioned stool. Mom was sitting beside him. They were sorting through the big black binder that always sat on the desk in the study. No one went into the study much. I had no interest in the business of the farm, and Mom and Dad weren't the types to sit at a desk.

"We invited the Hayeses over for supper tonight to discuss the dispersal sale," Mom said. Despite the history between Mike and me, dinner was appropriate given our families' long-standing relationship. "The whole crew is coming: Peter and Edith; Travis, Emily, and the three kids; their grandson Austin, who is staying with them for the summer; and Mike. We can't make you stick around, but your dad and I would like you to be here."

Before I could open my mouth, she added, "Running and hiding doesn't solve anything. You have no reason not to hold your head up high. At least think about it."

What was worse than the idea of sitting across from Mike as he had dinner with my parents was *not* sitting across from Mike as he had dinner with my parents. Maybe it was time to start being braver. After all, I wasn't being asked to be brave alone.

"Miah, I think we should talk about that calf again, too," Dad said.

"Mike killed him," I said, much more matter-of-factly than I felt. On the day Cutlet was killed, I had gone to Dad crying. Apparently, Mike had told him that the calf had taken a turn for the worse and couldn't stand up. Dad wasn't able to go out to the barn to check for himself, so he had trusted Mike. Calling the vet under the circumstances Mike had described would have cost more than the two hundred dollars the calf was worth.

"Was it lame?" he asked.

"No," I said. "He was fine when I fed him that morning."

I expected Dad to ask if it was possible that something had happened between when I had fed Cutlet and when Mike had found him, but this time he didn't.

"I'm sorry I didn't ask you before I gave Mike the go-ahead," he said instead.

"It wasn't your fault." I didn't know what to do with an apology. "Is now really a good time to talk about it, though, when they're all coming over for supper soon?"

"Now is the perfect time," Mom said.

Dad looked over his reading glasses at me. "We're going to clear up this business and start a new chapter for everyone."

I looked down at my fingers and fidgeted with my nails. I wondered what else Nathan had told Mom and how much Mom had told Dad.

I was curling my hair, applying makeup, and driving myself crazy playing out supper scenarios in my head when I heard Nathan singing. He danced his way into my bedroom, working his hips in ways that would have him sleeping on the porch if Dad saw him, no matter which team Nathan played for.

"Oh, come on!" he complained when I scowled at him. "We're going out tonight!"

"Yes, we are," I said, "after supper with the Hayeses."

Nathan wrinkled his nose. He had been supportive of my attending this supper, but he hadn't agreed to stick around himself. After I made it very clear that he was my getaway driver and had better be on alert for my text, he left with the keys to my Jeep.

I dressed in my only pair of designer jeans, which I had found at a thrift shop in Vancouver, and my first-date top. Nathan wasn't kidding about my being skinny. I was too skinny. These jeans were supposed to be tight. My salon highlights had grown out an inch, but time in the sun had lightened my roots and I had a natural look going for me. I wanted to look good. Why? Maybe to impress the Hayeses. Maybe to show Mike what he had lost. Maybe looking more attractive made me feel braver. But why did it take makeup, curled hair, and tight clothes? Was I more attractive this way to me because I was more attractive this way to others? Looking in the mirror, I realized that I was the same chicken I was in my rubber boots and ponytail. I was getting dressed up for the wrong reasons.

"Look at you all gussied up," Mom said when I entered the kitchen, making me question my choices even more.

"I will stay for supper, but not a second longer. Nathan and I are going to the city tonight," I reminded her.

She gave my shoulder a squeeze. I stirred the gravy wishing there was something more I could do to occupy my mind. Mike was on his way. I wasn't looking forward to seeing Travis with his cold shoulder or Austin with his roaming eyes, either. Did Emily hate me, too? The kids had been old enough to remember me. What had they been told about my abrupt exit from their lives?

The doorbell rang.

CHAPTER 33

EVERYONE ARRIVED AT ONCE, BUT IT HAD TAKEN TWO VEHICLES TO get them all down the road. Mom greeted the Hayeses as they filed in the door. There were a lot of shoes and coats, hugs and hair tussles. I hung back with a forced smile that I hoped passed as polite plastered on my face.

"Ray is in the dining room," Mom said. Edith and Peter said hello as they passed. The kids gave me curious looks as they shoved one another into the living room. Travis followed, reminding them to mind their manners and ignoring me completely. Emily, however, hugged me without hesitation. There was no better word to describe her than warm. Chestnut hair and brown eyes. She had always been soft-spoken but honest. I was beyond grateful, even if I wasn't a hugger.

"Mo-om," Emily's youngest son Graham called, and she was swept into the house.

Austin looked grim compared to the rest of the group, who wore colour and smiles. Even Mike smiled like the Mike my parents knew and hired, the Mike I had fallen for in high school.

Dad waited for everyone in the dining room, apologizing for not getting up. Somehow he had managed to pull on a pair of loose-fitting jeans. Unlike mine, his had been loose before he lost so much weight being in and out of the hospital; now they were almost comical. He sat at the head of the table with his leg propped on a cushioned stool, angled toward where Mom would be sitting.

Mom served a beef roast. The meal went well with light-hearted conversation about each family, Kingsley in general, and of course the weather. The plates were empty but not yet cleared when the men started talking about farming.

"So Mike, tell me again what was wrong with that calf we had penned in the barn," Dad said. I could feel my body tense. Mom continued to look at Edith, who was talking about her arthritis, but I could tell her ears perked, too.

"It was lame. The mama must have stepped on his right hind leg," Mike said.

"I thought you had said he wasn't getting better, that the electrolytes and medicine weren't helping," Dad said.

"That, too," Mike lied.

"With hindsight, I'm regretting not getting a second opinion," Dad said.

The other conversations in the room faded. The air in the room had changed. Everyone looked between Mike and Dad.

"Every rancher hates to lose a calf. Isn't that right, Peter?" Dad said at last, breaking the tension.

"Sure does," Peter said, from the opposite end of the table. He launched into a story about a lame calf from way back. Austin slumped, disappointed that normal conversation had resumed. I sneaked a look at Mike. Dad would have said he looked like someone had stuck a bicycle tire pump where the sun don't shine and puffed him up a bit. He wasn't as scary after some time apart and with my parents at my side, but when my eye caught his, I looked away quickly.

"Ray is looking like the day is getting long. Maybe we should get to business," Travis said as soon as Peter's story ended and before Peter could start another one. Dad was indeed looking paler than when supper had started.

Mom and Emily stood at the same time to clear the supper dishes. The men would talk business, and the women would make themselves scarce cleaning the kitchen. My mom and dad weren't the type to divide the sexes this way, but the Hayeses were. I felt disappointed in Mom for going along with it, then saw the look she and Dad exchanged. Clearing out the women and kids so Travis could talk comfortably was a decision they had made together.

"Can we play outside?" asked Graham.

"I want to play with the dogs," said Madison.

"You have grandchildren; I have dogs," Mom said with a laugh as she waited patiently for the older woman to get to her feet.

"Oh, did you see? Phyllis's granddaughter is having twins!" Edith said. "Serena was a grade below Miah, wasn't she?"

"Austin, go outside and play with your cousins," Peter said.

"Seriously?" Austin complained. "Why do I have to go with the little kids?"

"Stealing Grandpa's whisky from the liquor cabinet doesn't make you a grown-up," Peter said. That explained Austin's mood.

"Hey! Who are you calling a little kid? I wasn't the one scared of the steer today," Levi said. Austin made to grab for him, but Levi easily ducked out of the way. Peter laughed harder than anyone else. Austin peeled himself from the chair and followed his giggling cousins.

"The only one who treats me right around here is Uncle Mike," Austin said under his breath. I didn't think anyone else had heard, but Edith squeezed his hand as he walked by. "And you, Grandma," he said quietly. I doubted she was any consolation, but at least Austin had enough respect not to pull away from his grandma.

Emily and I washed dishes while Mom and Edith had coffee at the kitchen table. Emily asked questions about

Vancouver and school, but didn't say that she missed me or that she wanted me to come back.

"It's good to hear that you're doing so well," she said.

"Travis sure didn't seem happy to see me the other day."

"They're brothers. Mike has been filling his head with all sorts of stuff about you since you left. He wasn't mad that you left, though. He was mad that you came back," Emily said.

"Oh," I said, thinking that was worse.

Emily nudged me with her elbow. "Don't get me wrong. Mike can be a great guy and we love him, but before you left, we kind of thought he wasn't good for you. He changed you."

I wondered what Mike had filled Travis's head with. Travis had known me, still knew me. He shouldn't have believed Mike, brother or not. I realized then that even if I wrote the whole truth in the *Inquirer,* Travis would believe what he wanted to believe. And he would likely believe Mike.

Mom sent me into the dining room with the coffee pot and a plate of cookies. I was grateful because the suspense was making my stomach hurt. I wanted to know what was going on so that I could text Nathan and get out of there. Peter pushed his coffee mug in my direction. I had intended on setting the coffee on the table for the men to serve themselves, but I obliged and filled his mug. Then Travis's. Then Mike's.

"We need to shop around," Mike said as I worked my way around the table.

"These are more than fair prices on par with what Travis and I had discussed before cattle prices went up again," Dad said. "Any reason for the sudden change of heart?"

Dad seemed stiff, but I couldn't tell if he was frustrated with Mike or in pain. Maybe both. I filled up Dad's mug. He was the only one who thanked me.

"Maybe joining the herds sooner is better," Travis said, rubbing his chin. "We're pretty well set up for the expansion, with just the barn to finish up while the cattle are at pasture. That'll go quicker with Mike around now that the spraying here is done."

Peter didn't seem to be participating in the conversation much. He was there as a figurehead. His boys had been running the farm since his stroke.

"I don't mean to put pressure on you, Travis. I thought we'd meet to discuss it as neighbours. I will be able to manage combining, but with my leg as it is, ranching is too demanding. My other option is going to auction," Dad said. I doubted his doctors would agree about the combining, but I kept my mouth shut. "Judith and I are ready to sell the herd one way or another, and Miah wants to be a teacher, not a farmer. We don't want to be holding her here when she has a dream to chase."

Mike opened his mouth, but Travis lifted a couple fingers off the table as a signal to stop.

"No, no, I respect your having us here," Travis said.

"You boys are ambitious taking on nearly four hundred head. I had my hands full with half that," Dad said.

"If anyone can handle it, my boys can," Peter said. Dad nodded.

"Thanks, Ray. I will talk with Dad and my brother, but I think it's safe to start drawing up the paperwork. You're selling at a good time, and we can't complain. There's money to be had all around."

Feeling relieved, I made my exit. I pulled my phone out of my pocket and texted Nathan as soon as I was out of the dining room.

CHAPTER 34

WALK, WALK, WALK, I TOLD MYSELF AS I CROSSED THE PORCH AND descended the stairs. The Jeep was parked in the driveway with the engine running, Nathan at the wheel and Danika riding shotgun. I could hardly believe it. *Screw it, run!*

My smile couldn't get any bigger. Slightly out of breath, I yanked open the back door. I was even more surprised to find Alek scrunched in the tiny back seat.

"Did it go well?" Nathan teased.

"Yes. Let's get out of here before we jinx it." I slid in beside Alek.

"What are you guys doing here?" I was happy, mostly. Just a bit apprehensive. Was I going to get library Danika or Canada Day fireworks Danika? And had Alek come willingly this time?

"You'd better start driving before Mike sees us or I change my mind," Danika said. "I already miss my baby."

"So, where are the kids?" I asked.

"They have a father, you know."

I was impressed—and recalled that I had been impressed when Benton was a baby, too. A lot of guys we used to hang out with wouldn't have taken care of a toddler, let alone a baby, father or not.

"He works at the refinery tomorrow, though, so I have to be up with them no matter how awful early."

"That's right, *you* have to be up with them," Alek said, picking up on a conversation I wasn't a part of. Nathan started laughing, so it must have been part of the conversation that got them in the vehicle on the way to Edmonton with me.

"No," Danika said, "if Benton wakes up before Abby, I'm sending him your way."

"Poor Abby. I'd take my wingman over dealing with you hungover any day," he said. She turned and stuck her tongue out at him. They were closer now, I realized, with the differences of their youth behind them. I suspected the catalyst had been Danika's kids.

"What time does RC leave for work?" Nathan asked.

"Five a.m.," Danika said with a groan.

"Five o'clock curfew!" Nathan cheered and pumped his arm in the air. We all laughed.

"So you met RC?" I asked Nathan, curious how that went. RC, after all, was Mike's best friend, and none of Nathan and Mike's interactions would have encouraged me to show up at the fairy tale house.

"RC's never met anyone like Nathan." Danika giggled. "My husband doesn't do 'different.' It's why I never get to go to the theatre or try foreign foods, but at least I don't have to worry about him leaving me, right?"

"He made it about two minutes of awkward silence before turning up the TV," Alek said dryly. "If it's any consolation, I don't get much more."

"He's too funny," Danika said.

"More like rude," I muttered, my earlier fondness dampened. I squeezed Nathan's shoulder from the back seat, and he gave me an appreciative, lopsided smile in the rear-view mirror. I didn't mean to think of the *Inquirer,* but a potential headline popped into my head (**Phobics: They Don't Do Different**). It might have seemed perfect at one time, except I remembered Nathan's jokes about small-town living not so long ago (**When Stereotypers Become Stereotypees**). The *Inquirer* just didn't have the capacity to explore this topic properly.

"Earth to Miah," Danika said, interrupting my thoughts. She and Alek were both grinning at me.

"Hm?"

"I was just telling them about your eighteenth birthday, remember?"

Now that was a fun night.

"*My* Amiah rode the mechanical bull?" Nathan asked, encouraging Danika to go into detail about my "epic ride" and "cheering fans." Alek subtly shifted his knee so it pressed against mine. This was going to be a fun night, too.

After the minor issue of finding parking on a Saturday night, we stepped onto Whyte Avenue. A lively mosaic of bars, restaurants, and shops pressed together on either side. Our strange mix—Alek, Danika, Nathan, and I—wasn't so strange there. While passing a cowboy looking ready for the Calgary Stampede, we saw an elaborately tattooed woman wearing a live snake around her neck. There was no Mike, no *Inquirer*, no drama.

The days were long in the summer, so we started on the patio of a Mexican restaurant to enjoy the lingering sun. The other three ordered bulldogs, Coronas upturned in oversized slush margaritas. I volunteered to be the designated driver and helped myself to most of the shared nachos. Mom's beef roasts were always delicious, but I hadn't eaten much at dinner. This was the first time I had felt hungry in a long time.

We then made our way to an Irish pub, a sports lounge, a basement bar, a rooftop bar, and eventually a country saloon because Danika insisted that she needed to teach Nathan how to two-step.

By this time neither teacher nor student was sober. Amused, Alek and I watched from tall bar stools at a small table pressed against the railing surrounding the sunken dance floor. When the music shifted and they attempted the boot-scootin' boogie line dance, a man in worse condition than anyone else on the dance floor bumped into our table.

"This guy not know how to dance?" he asked, gesturing with his thumb toward Alek and eyeing me. It was an invitation, though not a very inviting one. The man was about thirty and no stranger to the gym, or at least some sort of upper-body labour. His aggressiveness and the smell of whisky made me freeze up. I managed an awkward shrug.

"Can't he talk neither? Some date," he said, now looking challengingly at Alek. Alek seemed unconcerned. Over his shoulder I saw two Saloon Security, their thumbs hitched in their belts and their eyes already trained on us. Neither looked as fit as my admirer, but they were sober and they had strength in numbers. Their walkie-talkies would quickly bring in reinforcements, if needed. I had seen it happen before.

"Didn't know you were talking to me," Alek said. "Besides, Miah can handle herself." He drank the last few swallows of his beer and stood. I worried he was going to leave me with this man the way he had with Mike at the fireworks. The string of line dances had ended, and aside from a few clusters of girls dancing together, the dancers were pairing off again. "But you make a good point. Miah, would you like to dance with me?"

On the drive back to Kingsley, Alek sat up front with me.

"I didn't expect you of all people to be able to two-step."

"Why me 'of all people'?"

"Country music, for one."

"The old stuff isn't all bad. Grandpa Leo always said I needed to know how to dance in order to court a young lady properly," Alek said, the corners of his mouth twitching as they did when he was amused. "Besides, it was a mandatory part of grade eight phys ed. Did you skip those classes? That would explain my bruised left foot."

"I must have. Are you offering lessons?" I peeked with my peripheral vision to confirm that he was looking at me the way he had been on the dance floor where we had gotten lost until last call.

"Ew," Danika interrupted. I blushed. I hadn't realized she was still awake. I glanced in the rear-view mirror. She was still eating take-out French fries behind me. Nathan had passed out with a half-eaten cheeseburger in his hand. "You two are actually cute together. It's disturbing."

CHAPTER 35

From: Concerned Citizen (concernedcitizen@freemail.com)
Sent: July 20, 2015 6:23:51 p.m.
To: Kingsley Inquirer (theinquirer@freemail.com)
Subject: Update

Anything yet?

From: Kingsley Inquirer (theinquirer@freemail.com)
Sent: July 20, 2015 8:01:21 p.m.
To: Concerned Citizen (concernedcitizen@freemail.com)
Subject: RE: Update

I have attached the five relevant emails so far. Three suggest Mike is responsible but have no supporting evidence. One offers car detailing services from one of our regular advertisers. And one is a gag claiming the missing garden gnomes spray-painted Alek's car. We can send you relevant emails as they arrive, but the contributions box at Kingsley Grocery isn't picked up until Friday.

From: Concerned Citizen (concernedcitizen@freemail.com)
Sent: July 20, 2015 8:30:47 p.m.
To: Kingsley Inquirer (theinquirer@freemail.com)
Subject: RE: Update

Not soon enough. I'll give you until Wednesday. If it's a problem, I will pick them up.

From: Kingsley Inquirer (theinquirer@freemail.com)
Sent: July 20, 2015 8:36:04 p.m.
To: Concerned Citizen (concernedcitizen@freemail.com)
Subject: RE: Update

No problem. I will get them to you by the end of day Wednesday.

The latest issue of the *Inquirer* had been out for only three days, and already Officer Petersen was demanding information. Nathan and I wanted to follow our Kingsley Inquirer Rules as closely as possible. Involving a police officer broke at least two of them. Rule two: stay neutral and anonymous. Rule six: don't let others do what you can do yourself (avoid third parties whenever possible). Allowing Bobby to pick up the contributions box would have raised suspicions. While police involvement may intrigue readers and increase sales, contributors and advertisers would be scared off, breaking two more rules. Rule seven: keep informants comfortable. Rule eight: keep advertisers happy.

All the deviations from our routine were worsening my anxiety, even if we were serving a good purpose. And I wasn't the only anxious one. I was annoyed that Nathan had had himself delivered to Kingsley instead of calling me. I chewed on my nails as Nathan tried reassuring Sanjit on the phone.

"I know you were contacted by a cop ... We aren't doing anything wrong. Freedom of speech is in the Canadian Charter of Rights and Freedoms ... What ride? ... I know what ride, Sanjit. I meant that I won't say you gave me a ride ... You don't have to explain anything to me. I totally understand. I can barely feed myself, let alone five kids ... So will you pick up the contributions box and send me a picture of the contributions before end of business day on Wednesday? We will pay you double the usual. It's just very important that we get the pictures before the stores close ... Thanks, Sanjit. You're the best."

We received the pictures on Wednesday afternoon as planned. I wondered whether Mr. Wong found the early pickup peculiar and whether he had mentioned it to anyone. What if we still didn't have whatever Bobby was looking for? Would we need to do another early exchange? The extra business expenses were adding up.

Nathan and I sorted the scanned files Sanjit had sent as well as the new pictures. The latest issues definitely had the town buzzing. We had twice as many contributions as usual. When we were done, we had eleven emails, two scanned files, and three pictures to forward to Bobby, but nothing useful as far as we could tell. I was attaching them to an email to Concerned Citizen when Nathan said he had missed one. I could tell he was happy and I hoped it was *the file*, the one Bobby needed. But this one belonged in the IT'S AMIAH folder. It consisted of two lines scribbled on the back of a receipt, likely for groceries that had been paid for moments before the note had been written. The receipt was for bananas, eggs, milk, and a case of canned stew, which was 20 percent off with the coupon in the latest issue of the *Inquirer.*

Mike should've kept it in his pants. He's lucky his heart is the only thing Miah broke.

The writing was familiar. I slipped out of the bedroom and down the hall. I was being quiet so I wouldn't disrupt the meeting in the dining room. Travis had returned alone to sign papers. I rounded the corner and gasped when I nearly ran into him.

"Sorry," he said in a gruff voice. "See you Friday."

Mom followed him to the door like a good hostess. I poked my head into the dining room where Dad was still looking over the contracts.

"All done?" I asked.

"All done," he said without looking up.

I was surprised how quick a dispersal sale could be. Within a few days Mom and Dad had met with their accountant; with Max Gilbert, the lawyer who rented office space from the bottle depot on Monday and Wednesday afternoons; and now with Travis. All made special trips to the ranch house because of Dad's leg. One of the perks to small-town living.

I turned back toward the kitchen.

"You're always on that computer of yours," Dad said, stopping me. "Can you do me a favour and write something for that *Inquirer?*"

I froze. "Uh, write something for the *Inquirer?*"

"Travis is buying the silage and vet supplies, but he doesn't need the feeders and some other things. I want to put a couple ads in the paper."

"Oh. No problem," I said. "Why don't you post them on buy and sell websites, too?"

He gave me a blank look.

"Online. If anyone is interested, they can email me," I said. His look didn't change, and I laughed. "Just a minute. I'll get my laptop and show you."

It felt good to be useful, and this time in a way that my parents wouldn't have thought of themselves. On my way to get my laptop, I remembered why I had emerged from my bedroom to begin with. I scanned the kitchen and snatched the grocery list off the refrigerator. I was right. My mom's writing matched that of the two-line message on the back of the receipt from the contributions box.

CHAPTER 36

"YOU'RE IN FOR A TRULY AUTHENTIC RANCHING EXPERIENCE TODAY," Dad said. Nathan gave him a skeptical look. We were all eating breakfast at the kitchen table at six a.m. The Hayeses—I wasn't sure which or how many—were due to arrive within the hour. It was Friday and we needed to prepare the herd to be moved, which meant dehorning, vaccinating, and branding.

Dad was in a great mood. Yesterday the doctor had put an ultra-light air cast on his leg. The infection hadn't returned, the cows were sold, and he was mobile for the first time in almost two months.

Breakfast consisted of bacon, sausage, eggs, hash browns, pancakes, and toast. A big breakfast meant a big day on the farm. I still didn't like mornings, but after a month of morning chores, I was used to waking up ridiculously early, unlike Nathan. Nathan's blond curls were matted on one side of his head and sticking out on the other. He wore pajamas and thick-rimmed glasses instead of his contacts. His chewing slowed and his bites grew further and further apart as he listened to Dad explain what had to be done. I think Dad had woken him up for entertainment.

"Castrating was the easy part. That's done in the spring when the calves are born," Dad said. "You take the bull calf, hold him down real tight because he ain't going to like this, and wrap a rubber band tight around his testicles. It cuts the circulation off, you see. Then, eventually, they just drop right off. Voilà, a steer!"

Nathan set down his toast and pushed his plate away. Dad burst out laughing, and even Mom giggled. Apparently, the cure for Nathan's nervous rambling was early mornings and ranching stories.

The morning air was still cool. Mike and Austin pulled up in Mike's pickup truck. Travis followed in his own truck, pulling an enclosed trailer. A lot of handshaking took place. Nathan and I hung back, shivering and quiet. I avoided looking at Mike. Inside the house I had been ready to help, but his presence made me feel foolish. Who was I to help with branding? I had never helped with branding in all the years I had lived on the farm, but I wasn't going anywhere. Austin winked in my direction. Nathan winked back. Austin's eyes got big and he turned away quickly, red-faced.

Dad wasn't well enough to be of any real use. I tried to compensate where I could. When asked, I ran for tools, water, food, or whoever or whatever else was needed. I wasn't good for much else, and I wondered if at times like these Dad would have preferred a son like Mike.

The Hayeses rounded up the herd with ATVs and separated the cows from the calves. Dad, Nathan, and I set up everything the Hayeses would need to vaccinate and brand the cows with their registered brand, a 2♥ on the left rear flank chosen by Peter and Edith when they first started out together. Before going back to the house to wait for the new homecare nurse, Dad gave me the wolf list. A dozen more items were crossed off. All were things that no longer needed to be done because of the dispersal sale. But at the end of the list were a couple new entries because of the dispersal sale.

• *Sell shoots, feeders, stock trailer, etc.*
• *Convert pasture*

The list was never-ending, but I understood it now and it no longer scared me. There was a new list in the notebook, an inventory of supplies included in the sale that needed to be loaded into the enclosed trailer. Nathan actually helped me this time. Loading the trailer was time-consuming. Only Dad understood his organized chaos. Maybe it made some sense to Mike after almost a year of working for Dad, but I wasn't about to ask.

Around noon, Travis hollered "Lunch time" as he and Mike passed the barn. Nathan and I followed, grateful for the break. Austin was limping, and his side was covered in dirt. Travis and Mike were teasing him about something. I was curious but didn't ask.

I wasn't surprised to see Peter sitting beside Dad at the dining room table. He wouldn't pass up a free meal. I waited until the Hayes men chose seats and then picked one as far from Mike as possible. The smell of burnt hair from branding clung to their clothes and lingered in the room. I breathed through my mouth as much as possible. With work still to be done, conversation was limited to requests for condiments and brief updates on the day's progress. The update included Austin's incident with a disgruntled cow. I would have liked to see him being spooked and running himself into the fence. Apparently, he was never in any real danger.

After lunch, Nathan and I finished loading the trailer with a pallet's worth of twenty-five-pound sacks of minerals and oats. Neither of us wanted to join the others at the shoots where the calves were bawling for their mamas and Mike was muttering about city boys and fairies. At least he had figured out that Nathan and I were just friends.

"Nathan, you're good at that computer stuff," Dad said. "If I showed you what needs to be sold, would you mind taking some pictures and posting some ads on that internet?" The obvious relief on Nathan's face made Dad chuckle.

"We didn't have these fancy electric branders in my day,"

Peter prattled as he followed. I was so grateful on Nathan's behalf that for a moment I didn't notice I was being left alone with Travis, Mike, and Austin.

Mike and Austin held the calves while Travis applied a paste that cauterized tissue and stopped the growth of the horns. If the horns were already too big, Travis used dehorners—which looked like giant nutcrackers—before applying the paste. Then he injected three different needles in the calves' necks or hips, depending on how the a calf was squirming around. Last, he pressed the electric brand to each calf's left rear flank. One Mississippi, two Mississippi, three Mississippi, four Mississippi, five Mississippi. The calves kicked and struggled, and sometimes branding took a couple of tries. Bruises for all those involved were inevitable. As devastating as it all seemed to an amateur, the calves scrambled to their feet and joined the cows as if nothing had happened. My job was to pass Travis tools as he needed them and to fill syringes.

"What are the pigs doing here?" Austin asked, interrupting our rhythm.

A police cruiser creeped through the bumpy field and parked in front of Mike's truck, which was backed toward the shoots. Cursing a particularly jumpy calf that got away due to the distraction, Travis pulled a hankie from his back pocket and wiped the sweat off his forehead.

"You two round up the next calf," Travis said to Mike and Austin. "Miah, I'm going to need more syringes."

I hesitated as Officer Peterson got out of the police cruiser, but he didn't give me more than a passing glance. I forced my feet to take me to the lowered tailgate of Mike's truck where the syringes and other supplies were. With my head bent over the syringes, I peeked up through my lashes. I saw Bobby and Travis shake hands in front of the police cruiser. After a few long minutes, Travis put his fingers in his mouth and pierced the air with a loud whistle, which made me fumble and drop a needle in the grass. If I wasn't careful, I was going to end up vaccinating myself. We all looked toward Travis, who waved Mike over. A couple minutes later, Travis returned to the shoots while Mike left with Officer Peterson. He sat in the front seat, not the back like the criminal he was.

"You're up, Miah," Travis said without looking at me. He grabbed another calf.

"What's going on?" Austin asked. Travis told him to help me hold the calf.

Eventually, Mike returned on foot, but not before I got my fair share of bruises. When the work was done and the sun hung low in the sky, we enjoyed Mom's three roasted chickens and the only tofu option she could find in town for Nathan. It was a sweet gesture. I smiled despite my aches and pains as Travis told Dad how well I had done. Nothing was said about Bobby's visit.

That night I couldn't wait to crawl into bed. I was exhausted but checked the *Inquirer* email inbox out of habit.

From: Concerned Citizen (concernedcitizen@freemail.com)
Sent: July 24, 2015 6:43:47 p.m.
To: Kingsley Inquirer (theinquirer@freemail.com)
Subject: RE: Update

Meet me tomorrow at 11:00 a.m., same place. Bring your partner.

CHAPTER 37

THE NEXT MORNING, I DIDN'T NEED TO GO OUT FOR MORNING CHORES since the cows were being hauled to the Hayes farm that day, but I was feeling sentimental. The toes of my borrowed rubber boots were wet from the dew and the air was cool, but I could already tell it was going to be a hot day. I lingered outside after counting fifty-nine 2♥s. The clocks weren't so loud out there. I sat on the fence and looked over the fields starting to turn gold.

I was no longer nervous turning my back on the cows. They were simply there, a fixture on the farm like when I was a kid. I wasn't feeling sentimental because ranching had grown on me, though I liked the firmer muscles I had noticed in my legs and arms even if I was a bit too skinny. Dad was healing; the cattle were sold, which was one less thing Mike could hold against me; and I felt like I had, for the most part, my friends and family back. I had more than survived my stay in Kingsley. I decided to drive back to Vancouver with Nathan the next day.

An eighteen-wheel semi-trailer truck lumbered up the driveway. I could see both Mike and Travis in the cab. They could take the whole herd at once with that size of cattle liner. The truck stopped in front of the house. Maybe Travis needed to talk to Dad or maybe it was only polite to stop in before loading up another man's cattle. I hopped off the fence and started toward the house. I was surprised when Travis headed in my direction.

"Everything okay?" he asked. I realized he hadn't expected to see me out there.

"Everything is great," I said. "Came out for morning chores out of habit, I guess."

He nodded, satisfied. Mike was digging in the toolbox of the semi, making a bunch of noise.

"Are you going back?" Travis asked.

"To the house? Yeah," I said. "I'll get out of your hair."

"No, back to Vancouver or wherever it was that you went."

"Oh," I said, feeling that sting again. "Yeah."

"Don't screw with Mike. He's still hooked on you."

"He has an odd way of showing it."

"I don't mean hooked on you in a good way." Travis was so serious. I knew then that he would never joke with me like he used to, but at least he was talking to me. I watched Mom round the truck and exchange a few words with Mike. There wasn't any friendly banter between them as there had been in June, either. They were polite but not friendly. Just like Travis and me.

Travis followed my eyes. "She'll be fine. Your parents are proud of you. We all are, so get out of here."

Travis and Mike moved the cattle liner, and Mom and I went inside to see what was delaying Dad when there were farm-related things to oversee. Yesterday, the new homecare nurse wasn't happy that Dad had been on his feet as much as he had been, but we didn't expect that to stop him today. The least we could do was drive him to the shoots.

"Hey, Dad, you're missing all the action," I called from the front door.

"Miah, can you come in here, please?"

I didn't like his tone and hoped that he hadn't hurt his leg again. Mom and I kicked off our boots and joined him in the living room. Nathan stood against the far wall looking at me with a sorry expression on his face. Dad was sitting on the couch with his eyes on my open laptop. I must have left it on the coffee table that morning. I couldn't see what was on the screen.

"What's going on?" Mom asked.

"I got a call about the old stock trailer," he said. It was one of the items Nathan had posted online for Dad.

"Oh, good," I said. Nathan shook his head slightly. Not good?

"The guy on the phone said that he had sent an email, so I went on your computer to check."

"Okay," I said. "Need help?"

"Your email was already open."

I instantly felt sick. My laptop was in the living room because I had been rereading Concerned Citizen's email while eating my oatmeal. I couldn't remember whether I had closed the email inbox. Even if I had, choosing the email icon would have automatically reopened the last account I had logged onto, which was for the *Inquirer*. Dad spun my laptop around so that Mom and I could see the screen. He was no longer looking at an email inbox but a working copy of the *Inquirer*. I was too stunned to look for my mom's reaction right away.

"What is that?" she asked, stepping closer for a better look.

"It appears our daughter and her friend here have taken up writing in their spare time," Dad said.

"You can't figure out a baby monitor or the TV remote, but you figured out how to find files on my laptop?" I blurted. Nathan shook his head a little more vigorously this time. I ignored him.

"I'm not stupid, Miah," Dad said, raising his voice. "Then again, I didn't know my own daughter was capable of this, so maybe I am."

"I didn't say you were."

"You implied it," he said, getting to his feet. He put too much weight on his injured leg and stumbled.

"Dad, you're going to hurt yourself." My eyes blurred with tears.

"I'm not worried about my leg. You have hurt me way more than my leg ever hurt. Me and almost everyone in this town!"

Tears started to roll down my cheeks. Nathan stared at the floor.

"This is done," Dad said, pointing at the laptop.

"It *is* done, Dad. I realized that this summer."

"We can't," Nathan said in almost a whisper. "It's not that simple."

"Why not?" Dad demanded.

"We took advanced payments from the advertisers, and we don't have the money to pay them back," Nathan said. It was my turn to be dumbfounded. "There were student loans and business expenses and—"

"Get my chequebook, Judith," Dad said. "How much?"

"No," I said. "You can't."

"How much?" Dad repeated.

"Probably about forty-five hundred," Nathan said. "I won't know for sure until we see what the last issue brought in."

Dad's eyes widened, but he didn't say anything. Mom returned from the study and handed Dad the chequebook for their personal savings account. He signed a blank cheque, using his thigh as a table. I was frozen in a state of shock with the *Inquirer* lit up on the laptop screen in front of me. Dad handed the cheque to Nathan, and Nathan took it.

"Make it go away," Dad said. He looked at me in a way he had never looked at me before. "All of it. You, too."

Dad dropped the chequebook on the coffee table and grabbed his crutches. The front door slammed behind him. Without saying a word, Mom picked up the chequebook and walked quietly from the room.

CHAPTER 38

I SHOULD HAVE BEEN OUTSIDE WITH MY DAD WATCHING THE CATTLE being loaded into the truck. Instead I was crying in my old bedroom. I couldn't stop. It was like all the anxiety of the summer was pouring out of my eyes and nose. The wastebasket was filled with crumpled tissues. I wasn't a pretty crier, which Nathan didn't need to point out but he did. Mom didn't bother checking in on us. She was cleaning. I heard pots clanging in the kitchen and then a little while later the vacuum cleaner humming in the living room.

"We used all that money to pay off my student loan, didn't we?"

"My flight, printing, extra deliveries ... it added up," Nathan said, but I knew that we had overextended because I was going to Kingsley for two weeks and didn't want to run into Mike before having paid off the student loan for which he had unknowingly co-signed. I sure hadn't expected to see him on the first day and in our driveway.

Neither Nathan or I had been foolish enough to think of the *Inquirer* as a long-term venture, and yet we had started counting on the income. I pictured Dad's face. The hurt and the anger. The disgust. Growing up, I had been the one to leave for school, leave for sleepovers at Danika's house, leave for summer camp. I had spontaneously moved out to live with Mike after high school and had moved to Vancouver. I had always been the one leaving, but also had always been welcomed back. My parents had always been there for me. Now they were telling me to leave. I had overstayed my welcome. I had never imagined that was possible.

The *Inquirer* needed to either fulfill advertising commitments or reimburse the advertisers. The money left in the company account and the proceeds from the current issue also needed to cover taxes and remittance. After crunching numbers, we confirmed that Nathan was right. If we folded the *Inquirer* right then, we needed four thousand five hundred dollars to break even.

"I have three thousand in my chequing account. It was my student loan we paid off, so it only makes sense that I replace the money," I said.

"Isn't that your tuition money?"

"I will take the semester off and save up for the winter semester. Rule eleven."

"There is no rule eleven."

"I'm making a rule eleven. Don't spend money you don't have."

Nathan looked as doubtful as I felt. We both knew I couldn't make that kind of money as well as pay for living expenses in that short time. And it wasn't likely that I would get another student loan, especially on my own.

"We have most of the next issue prepared. Do we finish one more? We can take a gamble and print extra copies, hoping the vandal story sells."

I shook my head. Rule ten: quit while you're ahead. When we had made that rule, we had meant know when to end an article or drop a story. We should have known when to quit the *Inquirer*.

At the truck stop diner, Officer Petersen was sitting at the same corner table as before. He was eating poutine Kingsley style—French fries topped with cheese curds and gravy—and flipping through the latest issue of the *Inquirer*.

"Cops are trained to sense fear like a dog," Nathan whispered. "We don't want him thinking we are scared."

"I *am* scared," I whispered back.

Bobby didn't say anything as we joined his table.

"Can I get you anything?" the same teenaged waitress as before asked.

"Just water, please," I said. She looked irritated. Water didn't earn tips. I was too nervous to eat anything, though, and anything with caffeine wasn't good for my already high anxiety. Nathan ordered an iced tea.

We waited in silence until the waitress served our drinks. Then Bobby wiped his mouth with a napkin and sat back in his chair.

"Rough morning?" he asked, taking in my swollen red eyes.

"You could say that. Dad found out about the *Inquirer*," I said. Nathan and I had decided it wouldn't hurt if Bobby knew he wasn't the only one who knew our secret. It would possibly take some power away from him. "I'm sorry we weren't much help with your case."

"You were," Bobby said. "We found yellow spray paint hidden in the spare tire in the box of Mike's truck that matched the spray paint on Alek's car."

"I knew it," said Nathan.

Spray-painting MIAH'S BITCH on Alek's car when the *Inquirer* had just published an article that would make Mike the obvious suspect didn't seem like Mike's style. He liked to work in the grey area. I pictured him slipping out of the bar unnoticed for a half hour. Was it two years of pent-up anger fueled by alcohol and seeing me with another guy—two, if you count Nathan—that made him sloppy? Maybe RC had been an accomplice. Would he have trashed his own brother-in-law's car? The article for the *Inquirer* was writing itself in my head, a reflex in the tabloid business where quick turn-arounds were pivotal.

"It wasn't Mike," Bobby said. "It was the nephew defending Uncle Mike's honour while drunk on Grandpa Pete's whisky."

"Austin!" I imagined his teenage eyes travelling up and down the length of my body. I could picture him spray-painting the car and smashing the windshield and headlights. I could imagine Mike's role, too: encouraging his troubled nephew while maintaining deniability. That was Mike's style.

"Petty crimes are why Claire sent Austin to Kingsley for the summer. She was hoping some positive male influence and tough love from Peter and Travis could straighten him out. I had my suspicions it was him."

"If you had your suspicions, why did you need the *Inquirer*?"

"The article gave me a reason to approach the Hayeses without outright accusing anyone. They agreed to a search without a warrant knowing I could get one because of the article. If nothing turned up, they would have been just a couple more people mad at the *Inquirer*."

"So you needed the article, but didn't need the emails," Nathan said. Bobby looked at him for a couple seconds before answering.

"It's my job to explore every angle," he said at last. "Alek has decided not to press charges. Travis is going to pay for the damages and have Austin work off the debt on the farm. Case closed."

I hadn't seen Alek since the night we introduced Nathan to Whyte Avenue. Was it only a week ago that we had danced until our feet ached? We had talked a couple times on the phone, me sitting in Mom's kitchen twirling the cord of the outdated phone between my fingers, but not since branding, when Bobby had collected Mike to search his truck.

"Now," Bobby said as he tapped the cover of the *Inquirer* and regained my focus.

"We're done with that," I said.

"That's it? I feel cheated. I had all these arguments prepared on how these types of papers don't work in small towns. How you're going to get sued or get the snot kicked out of you by some angry country boys," he said. He looked pointedly at Nathan.

"Well, we're almost done," Nathan said hesitantly. "We need to print one more issue. We already accepted money for advertising and people are relying on the calendar." The last argument sounded weak now that we were in front of a police officer.

"You wouldn't want to leave your readers hanging on the vandal story either," Bobby said dryly. He looked at us for a moment, thinking it through, I assumed. "And I hear Trula and Roland are back together."

Nathan opened his mouth, but I kicked him under the table.

"Last time we met, you said that you never had these problems at the station or at home when the *Gazette* was reporting the local news," I said.

"The *Gazette* didn't sell eight hundred copies every two weeks or help solve crimes either," Nathan muttered.

"You sell how much every month? And collect for advertising?" Bobby broke his cool façade for the first time. I glanced at the waitress, who was so bored she didn't even try to look like she hadn't overheard the outburst.

"Jack Whitby, your father-in-law, was the publisher of the *Gazette,* right?" I asked in a low voice.

Bobby leaned forward and folded his hands on the table. We had his attention. After we finished our proposal, Bobby agreed to one more issue. He stood to leave, tucking the *Inquirer* under his arm and pulling ten dollars out of his pocket for his bill.

"I know your dad, Miah," he said. "He's a reasonable man. Make sure he sees that the tabloid wasn't all bad. I'll give you the same advice I gave Austin yesterday, though. If you can't show your face or tell the truth about what you're doing, maybe it's not all good either. I'll be in touch."

CHAPTER 39

NATHAN AND I STUFFED THE LUGGAGE INTO THE BACK OF MY JEEP. There was no tearful, touching goodbye scene. Dad stayed in the house. Mom sat on the porch steps with the dogs panting at her feet after a vigorous game of fetch, just like the day I had arrived. As I backed up to turn around in the driveway, Nathan rolled down the passenger-side window.

"Thanks for everything," he called. Mom waved.

As we pulled away, Nathan watched the farm fade in his side-view mirror. Kingsley was more than a set with a cast of characters to him now. Well, at least the farm was.

Nathan reviewed everything we had already reviewed a hundred times over the last twenty-four hours. Eventually, he gave up talking. We listened to the radio until I pulled into the departures drop-off zone at the airport an hour later.

"You sure?" Nathan asked.

"I can't keep running away." Those words had become my mantra. *I can't keep running away. I can't keep running away. I can't keep running away.* "Remember, I'm going to write the feature and you're going to print it the way I send it this time, okay?"

"Don't write anything stupid," Nathan said. He gave me a hug across the middle console before hopping out of the Jeep and grabbing his duffle bag from the back seat.

When I got back to the farm, my heart, head, and fingers ached. I had chewed my nails too short. Mom and Dad must have been outside somewhere because the house was still. I lay on my bed and soon fell asleep. When I woke up from one nightmare, I rolled over and had another. I heard the phone ring a couple times but didn't care who called. No one called me for dinner. My stomach growled, but I had no desire to eat. Eventually, everything was dark. Mom and Dad must have gone to bed.

My nightmares since Concerned Citizen's first email were similar to the ones I had had before I ran away from Kingsley and for quite awhile after. They were of my parents abandoning me. Of being replaceable and Mike saying, "I told you so." Of Mike cheating on me with Danika or Tamara or the teenage waitress from the truck stop. Sometimes Mike would morph into Alek, who would also cheat on me. Of Alek being disgusted that I was the co-publisher of the *Inquirer.* Of Nathan blaming it all on me. Of the town turning on me and my parents and one another with torches at night like in an old horror film. Of being sued and losing the farm. Of going to jail and never having a single visitor.

The worst was the return of a recurring dream from my days living with Mike.

I tried talking to Mike, my mom, my dad, Danika, even the lady who worked at the post office ... but the words wouldn't come out.

My chest tightened up and my breath came short. I was having a panic attack. People looked at me like I was a little kid throwing a tantrum over a chocolate bar Mommy wouldn't buy her in the grocery store.

"Smarten up," my mom said.

"Smile, Miah," my dad said. "You have such a pretty smile."

Mike winked at me, which was the point in the dream when I discovered that my tongue had been cut out. I couldn't talk.

I hadn't had that dream since Nathan and I started the *Inquirer*. I couldn't go back to the way it was. I couldn't.

In the morning, I felt good for about thirty seconds. That's how long it took for reality to wash over me. Lying there staring at the ceiling and feeling like an ice cream scoop had been used to hollow out my insides, I wasn't surprised to smell baking bread. Mom worked when she was upset. I rolled out of bed, worried that if I didn't, the pattern would be scrubbed off the dishes, the freezers would be overflowing with baked goods and casseroles, and the vacuum cleaner would burn out. Also, I was tired of people making decisions for me.

Mom was in the kitchen. The cupboards were clean and the sink was shining.

"Baking bread in the heat of summer. What was I thinking?" she said. She wiped the back of her hand across her forehead. The room was already like a sauna with the oven on, and we hadn't even reached the hot part of the day yet. "I'm going out to the garden. Are you coming?"

"Sure," I said, grabbing a bun. I was going to make a conscious effort to fix my weight.

We busied ourselves weeding between the rows in the garden and filling a ten-gallon bucket with produce ready to be eaten, stored, canned, or blanched.

"I said it once and I will say it again: I acted perfectly fine that day at the store," Mom said.

"I know, Mom. It wasn't meant to ..."

"I have a few questions," she said. I braced myself for a lecture. "Are you Deirdre? Where did you get that strawberry–rhubarb tart recipe? And do you know who stole the baby Jesus? Because Edith says it was the Plunket boy and I just can't believe that. And where do you get all this information? Some of it is entertaining, I'll give you that much. Maybe

Education isn't the right choice for you."

"Believe me, it is. I'm not cut out for the newspaper business."

"I was thinking more along the lines of fiction writing," she said, giving me a stern look.

For the next three days, I followed her around as she did her chores and I talked. I told her about my old life in Kingsley and about my new life in Vancouver. As memories and thoughts hit me, I blurted them out loud. I told Mom about Mike getting drunk and forgetting my twenty-second birthday and about trying to be perfect so he wouldn't replace me. I even told her about when he drank and no didn't mean no, but he was always really sorry if he remembered. I told her about wanting to do something more with my life. I even admitted that I had thought about how convenient the schedule as a teacher would be if I ever did have children of my own. These things didn't need to be in print, but they needed to be said. She didn't have to ask too many questions once I had started talking. She did have a few more, though.

"Mom!"

"What?" She laughed. "There was a picture of you and Alek kissing in the dirt, oblivious to people taking pictures twenty feet away from you. 'Is Alek a summer fling or a pros-pect?' is a valid question. The boy has called the house twice since Nathan flew home, and as far as I know you haven't called him back."

The notepad by the phone also said Mike had called. She didn't question my not calling him back.

Dad still didn't say more to me than *Morning, Pass the salt*, and *G'night*. In the evenings, I worked on my share of the final *Inquirer* articles in the living room while Mom knitted. Dad sat on the porch and went to bed early. He didn't even join us when I tried luring him in by putting the football game on TV.

"He'll come around," Mom said.

CHAPTER 40

ON WEDNESDAY NIGHT, MOM WAS SITTING ON THE COUCH KNITTING and I was still struggling with the feature article for the last issue of the *Inquirer.* Usually I didn't have time to waste over one article. In Vancouver I had classes, homework, the bistro, and a social life to work around. Back at the Kingsley pace of life, I wondered how I had once fit it all in. After reading and rereading professional tabloids to develop the voice, the articles had come easily, though. Especially when I hadn't cared about the content and no one had known I was the one who was writing it. My phone vibrated.

    Nathan: Check the email

I opened the *Inquirer* inbox.

    From: Concerned Citizen (concernedcitizen@freemail.com)
    Sent: July 29, 2015 7:52:21 p.m.

To: Kingsley Inquirer (theinquirer@freemail.com)
Subject: Gazette Terms & Conditions

Jack agrees to your proposal, but I would like to clarify and emphasize the following:

1. Circumstances surrounding the Kingsley Inquirer and the Inquirer's cancellation will remain confidential. (Disguised under 'police business' when/if necessary.)
2. Advertising will carry over from the Kingsley Inquirer.
3. All proceeds from the reformed Gazette will go to you until your debt is paid off. Then all proceeds will go to Jack until you have reached equilibrium.
4. Herein the two parties will come up with systems and roles for operating the reformed Gazette.
5. I no longer have to deal with this and can watch football in peace.

Jack: 780.555.6891 / jack_p_whitby@freemail.com

I didn't care if Mom was in the same room. I called Nathan as soon as I was done reading.

"We need this last issue of the *Inquirer* to sell and sell big. Then we're out, Amiah," Nathan said. "We'll add a few extra pages for what we would have printed in August, like the calendars. I've already contacted all the advertisers, and most are keeping the ad space they've already paid for despite the month delay. Some are even paying for bigger ads, cashing in on the farewell issue. If sales are good for the new *Gazette*, they will buy more. We're good at this."

"No, you are. I don't have the nerves for it."

"The *Gazette* won't be so bad," he said. "You know, if we do this right and hold off on paying your dad back for just a little while, you can still come back to school this fall. We can go together. My transfer into the Journalism program was accepted!"

"That's great," I said, mustering as much cheer as I could. There wasn't much cheer to muster. I felt trapped again, but this time I had only myself to blame. "I'm happy for you."

Mom's knitting needles continued to click, but I knew she was listening. I covered the mouthpiece on the phone and whispered Nathan's news. She gave me a thumbs-up.

"Don't let the black hole suck you in," Nathan said. "We can live together to save on rent like we talked about. You know your parents would do anything to help you out, and it's not like you won't ever pay them back."

I wasn't so sure. Dad wasn't talking to me. And making it on my own was one of the only things I was proud of. "I'll think about it."

"You can pay part of your rent in baking for all I care. I need to renew my gym membership after my Alberta vacation," he said. I listened to him excitedly ramble about his courses and all the things we could do on campus this fall. The conversation didn't require much input on my end. "Seriously, though, Amiah, don't give up. Let your friends and family help. Not everyone has ulterior motives and expectations to blindside you with. We aren't all Mike."

A few minutes after I hung up the phone, Dad paused in the entranceway of the living room, saw that I was there, and turned to leave.

"You can watch TV, Dad," I said.

"Are you working on that paper?" he asked.

"Yes. I have to finish the last issue. I can work somewhere else, though. It's your house, your TV."

"It's fine. I'll go read."

"I got another email about the stock trailer," I said quickly before he could leave.

"Get a number. Talking on the phone is easier than dealing with the computer." He stepped away.

"Dad!" My voice was louder and harsher than I had meant. I was desperate. "Quit giving me the cold shoulder. Yell, scream, whatever you need, but enough with the silent treatment. That's what Mike used to do, okay? Sometimes for days. I can't handle it." My eyes blurred with tears, and there was a catch in my throat.

"I have nothing more to say."

"What? Are you going to make me beg, too?" He hadn't

wanted to hear that, to know that. His shoulders slumped and he pinched the bridge of his nose. Mom's knitting needles went quiet. Mom looked at him with raised eyebrows, willing him to stay put and listen. "I left because I couldn't handle it. I didn't want to come back. I missed home and you and Mom and Danika and the stars and ..." I wiped my eyes and nose on my sleeve. "I just couldn't be Mike's Girl anymore. That's all I was in Kingsley."

"What about my girl?" Dad asked. "You were my girl first."

I slumped. "I was his property, Dad. Inside and out. I couldn't explain it then, and I'm not saying the way I started finding my voice again was right, but I'm trying to make up for it now." As my mind raced in search of the right words, my chest felt tighter and my breath grew shorter. The search was hopeless, so I said what had been bothering me since the day I had returned to Kingsley. "I came back and he was here. Mike was here, smiling and winking like he was right all along. I was replaceable. Only you were happy to see me and now ..." I was having trouble breathing.

Mom set her knitting down. "Where are your pills, Miah?" she asked in her calm, steady way.

We weren't a touchy-feely family on the Williams farm. We hadn't needed to be to know what we thought of one another. But that day I needed my dad to hug me. And he did.

"Quit trying to make the town get you, Miah," he whispered with his arms around me and his cheek resting on the top of my head. "Cinderella's cowboy boot is too small. You outgrew this place. But that's not saying it's not perfect for anyone else. Like me and your mother."

STREETS SAFE AGAIN

Car vandal caught ... who did it and why?
How the town came together to right a wrong

KINGSLEY
INQUIRER

NATURAL SUNBURN REMEDIES

GOING, GOING, GONE!

THE INQUIRER SOLD

IS THE REPLACEMENT THE INQUIRER IN DISGUISE?

GREY-HOUND ROLLS OVER

Kingsley Volunteer Rescue First on Scene

Kissing Cousins
'We didn't know we were related!'

REUNITED
Roland and Trula settle differences
outside of court

$2.00
July 31, 2015

CHAPTER 41

I TOOK A DEEP BREATH AS MOM PARKED THE CAR ON MAIN STREET. Kingsley Grocery was especially busy, even for the lunch hour on the day the *Inquirer* was released. Out front, four giggling teenage girls circled around a copy of the newspaper. They were oblivious to the people who had to walk around them to get in or out of the store. A farmer, a teacher, Trula, a ten-year-old kid, Emily ... each left the store with a copy of the *Inquirer*. The main headline had everyone's attention: **Going, Going, Gone! The Inquirer Sold**

"Sidewalks are for walking. Move it, girls," Baba said, her cane stuck out in front of her. The girls made a path for Baba. No one doubted they would otherwise be jabbed with the rubber foot of the cane. Danika followed, pushing her fancy jogging stroller.

"Sorry," Danika apologized to the girls.

"Don't be," Baba told her. As soon as they had passed, the girls reformed their circle.

"Hello," Mom said at the same time as I said, "Hi, Baba."

"The Williamses, too? Did the whole town run out of milk today?"

"The *Inquirer* was released today," Mom said, "and I hear it's the last one."

Danika's jaw dropped, and she gave me a look that screamed *What?!?* She gripped the stroller to keep from running into Kingsley Grocery and buying a copy right then.

"Good riddance," said Baba.

Danika changed the subject before Baba could rant about the newspaper. "Abigail and I thought we'd visit Grandpa at the manor during our lunch break, and we ran into Baba."

"I was seeing about a job in the kitchen, but it's been filled," said Baba. "I'm going to be teaching a cooking class at the Senior Centre instead. Young girls today don't know how to make a good, old-fashioned meatloaf, shepherd's pie, pierogi, or cabbage roll, right, Judith?"

Mom agreed.

"We are on our way back to the library to figure out the details," said Danika, looking less determined than Baba. "You know, you're going to need posters to advertise. Alek is at home with Benton. Maybe you should ask him to help you this afternoon. He is an artist and graphic designer. That's the sort of thing he does for a living."

"Good idea. I already know exactly what I want," said Baba. Danika and I smiled, both imagining unsuspecting Alek's afternoon. "You're going to have to sign up quick, Miah, before the class fills up."

"Thanks, Baba, but I leave for Vancouver tomorrow. I have to be back for pre-registration and open house at the University," I said.

"What makes those classes better than my classes?" Baba asked.

"They aren't better," I said, quickly. "I'm getting my teaching degree, though."

"We will both be teachers! Good for you. After, come over for a sleepover. You girls haven't had a sleepover in a long time. But enough idle chitchat. Bye for now," said Baba. She continued toward the corner where the crosswalk led to the library.

"Get me a copy," Danika whispered to me. She pulled a toonie out of her pocket, pushed the coin into my hand, and followed Baba.

Kingsley Grocery was as busy inside as outside. Mom dropped a toonie into the contributions box and picked up her copy of the *Inquirer*. I already knew we would be buying toilet paper and dry pasta. She flipped to the coupons, which were for a dollar off toilet paper and buy two, get one free on dry pasta.

"Let's make Rice Krispies squares this week instead," Mom said, as we passed the bananas. There was enough banana bread and cookies in the freezer to last until Christmas. She added a gallon of milk and a box of Rice Krispies to the red basket I carried to the till.

"I only know that a new newspaper is coming," Mr. Wong told two women who were paying for groceries when we joined the line. "Come again and you will see."

I hadn't thought about how Mr. Wong would be affected by the *Inquirer*'s demise. He had relied on the newspaper to draw business. Other businesses in the area relied on the advertising. Organizations, the calendar. Bobby was right: it wasn't all bad.

When Mom and I got home, Dad was sitting on the porch editing the wolf list. I opened the *Inquirer* to the page I wanted Dad to read and set it on the little table beside him before I went inside. I had no idea what he would think, but he needed to read it and I couldn't stand there watching as he did.

ADIOS INQUIRER

After seven spellbinding months the *Inquirer* is closing the doors! But we have to let you in on a little secret first. It can't ever really end when we never printed anything you weren't already talking about. All of our sto-ries started with a slip on Facebook, a whisper in the café, a public scene ...

Love it or hate it, the *Inquirer* taught us all some things. Everybody talks. There are at least two sides to every story, some less true than others. And every story is eventually replaced by another and then another.

The *Inquirer* sees no better way to wrap up than with some reviews from some of our more articulate anonymous contributors.

• 'When I am looking at magazine stands, my eyes are always drawn to the headlines of the tabloids. Celebrities, politicians, and business gurus are at the mercy of the press. The *Inquirer* is an awesome social experiment, subjecting regular people to the limelight!'

• 'This stuff needs to stop. You're prying into people's personal business.'

• 'Putting this s**t in print makes people think twice about what they say. Good on them.'

• 'The *Inquirer* makes people confront things in a way they wouldn't normally. It's the agent of change in a small town where little changes.'

• 'The *Inquirer* makes small-town drivel funny. I actually read the newspaper now.'

• 'This is an abuse of our right to freedom of speech. If we wanted to live this way, we would move to Los Angeles and mingle with the Hiltons and Kardashians.'

• 'I don't get what the big deal is about the *Inquirer*. It's just a newspaper. If you don't like it, don't read it. I don't.'

• 'We want the *Gazette* back!'

Thank you to all our readers and advertisers! Let's all remember to think twice before we open our mouths to speak or our laptops to tweet!

I had written and rewritten a hundred versions of that article. I had tried to explain the *Inquirer's* creation, motivation, and destruction. I had tried to apologize for any damage done, but also justify our actions. One version I wrote was a tell-all, revealing myself and taking responsibility, as Nathan feared I would. The backlash on my family, the town, and me wouldn't have been worth it, though. People knowing who was behind the *Inquirer* wouldn't change the rumours or make up for the *Inquirer* helping circulate the rumours. I realized that none of these versions of the article would work because none could be written in the voice of the *Inquirer,* which had become a living, breathing presence apart from Nathan and me. Danika's letter would never be printed, but it inspired my final article. 'There is a time to speak up and a time to be quiet.' It was the *Inquirer's* time to be quiet.

Dad knocked on my open bedroom door and tossed the *Inquirer* onto the bed.

"This reads like any other article in the *Inquirer,* but I get it. We aren't going to agree and we've each said our piece," he said. "Be back for Thanksgiving, okay? Your mother and I are going to miss you."

"Okay," I said, breaking into a smile. "Thanks, Dad."

CHAPTER 42

SOMEONE KNOCKED *RAT-A-TAT-TAT* ON MY BEDROOM WINDOW. I opened my eyes and waited for them to adjust to the dark. Had I dreamt it? Then there was another *rat-a-tat-tat*. My heart started hammering in my chest. I slipped out of bed, wearing my tank top and pajama pants, and peeked out the window. Mike looked back at me with a cocky smirk on his face. I opened the window just enough for us to be able to hear one another.

"Just like old times, eh?" he said. I could smell the whisky on his breath. He started to lift the window higher, and I stopped it.

"No, not like old times," I said. If it were old times, one of us would be helping the other in or out. I was grateful for the barrier between us now. I would scream before I let Mike through that window. Then I realized I couldn't scream. Dad would jump to his feet and hurt himself. I could call out for Mom. All the possible scenarios ran through my head. "What do you want, Mike?"

He suddenly hit the side of the house with his hand.

"I called you. Twice."

"I've been busy. Dad said you were stopping in this week-end for your paycheque, so I thought we could talk then."

"I can't get that kiss from the other day out of my head. I know you can't either," Mike said.

"Yeah, but for different reasons."

Mike's face scrunched up, and he swayed a bit. "You can't afford to be lippy, Miah."

"The sale is done. I will be gone tomorrow. We've both moved on with our lives," I said.

"I received an interesting letter in the mail. It says that my loan has been paid off and it thanks me for my business. I called the bank to let them know there's been a mistake because I didn't have a loan," Mike said. My stomach did a flip. He was only a co-signer, and I had made sure to receive all the mail for the loan electronically. I didn't realize that he would be notified when I paid it off. "Then I had a little chat with Max Gilbert. You know, the lawyer."

I looked down at my bare toes. The pink toenail polish was half grown out. I could use a pedicure. It would be fun to go with Danika. Had I actually thought I was going to be able to leave Kingsley so easily a second time?

"It was a student loan," I said. "I paid it off."

"I asked Max Gilbert what would happen if someone forged a signature to get a loan. Fraud charges in Alberta are a two-thousand-dollar fine and can land you in jail for six months."

"Good thing I've never forged a signature in my life and don't have to worry about it, then," I said. I wasn't anxious. I was angry.

Mike had smelt like whisky the night he signed the forms, too. He hadn't asked what the forms were for. It was his own fault he had assumed they had to do with his bills. He should have organized his own bills instead of expecting me to, and I shouldn't have tried so hard to please him all the time.

"There's that lip again," Mike said. "I don't remember you being so lippy when we lived together."

"You should go home. It's cold and late," I said.

"Don't tell me what to do."

"I'm not," I said. "Wait. Maybe I am. Go home, Mike."

He hit the house again and then started to pace. "You haven't got your head on straight."

The bathroom light across the hall lit up my bedroom. Mike stepped back into the dark.

"Miah? What are you doing?" Mom asked.

There was a time to speak up and a time to be quiet.

"Mike's here," I said.

"Bitch," Mike said under his breath. Despite logic, it stung. Mike had been my first love, whether it was true or not. He knew me in ways no one else did because I hadn't let anyone get that close to me again. That knowledge had given him power over me.

Mom came into my bedroom and looked out the window.

"What's going on, Mike?" she asked.

"Nothing, Judith. Go to bed."

"You've been drinking," she said, frowning at him.

"I'm almost thirty, remember?"

"Yes, so you're old enough to know better. Did you drive here?"

Mike hesitated enough to confirm that he had. He had parked halfway down the driveway so he wouldn't wake up my parents, like in the old days.

"You better get home," Mom said. "Leave the truck."

I closed the window on his sour face before he could respond. Mike spat on the side of the house before turning away. He tripped on his own feet but caught himself. I had seen enough and closed the curtains.

CHAPTER 43

I WOKE AGAIN TO KNOCKING ON MY BEDROOM WINDOW. MY EYES popped open. Not again. I slipped out of bed for the second time that night. I picked up my cell phone off the nightstand, prepared to call the police. Let Officer Petersen deal with Mike. My nerves were like live wires as I opened the curtains, bracing myself to see Mike.

When I looked out the window, I found Alek instead. Didn't the men in Kingsley know what a door was for? Or a clock? It was midnight. Less than an hour had passed since my last impromptu visitor. I dropped my phone on the bed, resisted the urge to check my bed hair with my hands, and opened the window.

"Sorry. I didn't want to wake your parents by knocking on the door or calling the house. I would have texted you, but I'm not privileged enough to have that number," Alek teased. He kept a straight face, but I knew his tells.

"Was Mike's truck in the driveway?"

"No. Should it have been?"

"Long story," I said. I didn't want to talk about Mike, though. And I definitely didn't want Alek to get the wrong idea about Mike and me again. "What are you doing here?"

"Come out and see."

I had promised myself an hour ago when Mike had stood at the window that I wasn't going to make the same mistakes. Alek recognized my internal conflict. How could he not? In a matter of seconds, I bit my bottom lip, ran my hand through my hair, glanced at my bedroom door past which my parents slept, and crossed an arm protectively over my stomach.

"We'll be on our best behaviour. Scout's honour," he said. He covered his heart with his right hand. I wasn't sure what the actual Scout salute looked like, but I was pretty sure that wasn't it. "The northern lights are visible, and they are one of the things I actually miss about living in the sticks."

This was different. I pulled on my UBC hoodie and wrote a quick note to leave on my bed. Twenty-five years old or not, I didn't want to worry Mom more than I already had if she happened to wake up again. I used the front door instead of climbing out the window, too.

Alek waited for me at the bottom of the porch steps. We didn't go far. We passed his car, which he had parked up the drive and in front of the house like a normal person. In the grass beside where we had painted the fence together, Alek had laid out a blanket and two juice boxes.

"Benton's grape juice was the closest thing I could find to wine at my sister's house," he said. "I forgot that everything in Kingsley is closed by six o'clock."

"It's perfect," I said. "You lucked out. The northern lights are a super-smooth way to pick up a girl. Grandpa Leo would be impressed."

"Wasn't luck. There's a website: one for picking up girls and one following the northern lights. I was keeping my eye on the northern lights one this time. The site tracks them and uses percentages for optimal viewing times based on location. Today's percentage for the Edmonton area is the highest it has been all summer," he said.

We lay side by side on our backs. The sky was streaked with wavering green, blue, and white lights, looking like an artist had made enormous, shimmering brushstrokes on a water canvas. I had lived in Kingsley almost my entire life and the only notice I had paid to the northern lights was identifying them on a multiple-choice science test in elementary school. They were beautiful.

"I've been wanting to do this since Canada Day," Alek said. "The northern lights were cutting it a little close since Danika said you're leaving tomorrow. She also told me which window to knock on. Reluctantly."

"I'm heading home," I said.

"Home?"

"Vancouver for now. That's where all my stuff is anyway. I don't fit here," I said. He unlaced his hands on his stomach and rested one in the middle between us. An invitation. I accepted. His fingers were long and warm as they wrapped around mine. "What about you? How long does it take to fumigate an apartment building?"

"Renovate. And not this long, but I had to wait for the northern lights. They aren't the same in the city. The pollution and lights get in the way."

"Admit it. Bad Boy Alek would rather hang out with his two-year-old nephew."

"Him, too," Nathan said. "As for the 'Bad Boy' part, you shouldn't believe every rumour you hear. Besides, I'm all grown up now." He squeezed my hand, and we lay there awhile in our comfortable silence.

"Nathan and I were the ones behind the *Inquirer*," I said.

"And I'm the one who stole the baby Jesus and the garden gnomes," Alek said.

"No, you aren't. Warren Plunket and his punk friends did."

Alek burst out laughing. He rolled onto his side and propped himself up on his elbow so that he was hovering over me with the northern lights glimmering behind his head.

"You're serious? Even the Miah the Man-Eater bits?"

"Well, Nathan started that."

Alek didn't back away from me in disgust like in my dream. He laughed. His laugh was infectious, and I found myself laughing, too.

"I thought you didn't read the *Inquirer*," I said.

"There's nothing else to do in this town. Plus, I was on the cover with a hot girl who has a hot-tempered ex. How could I not read it? I know I'm amazing, but I'm still human," he said. "So what possessed you to start the *Inquirer*?"

"Opportunity, money, entertainment ... because I'm messed up," I said, answering as honestly and clearly as I ever had before. It was easier with Alek somehow. Nathan had been wrong when he had said it was because Alek didn't matter, though. I didn't feel anxious around him.

"Ever going to tell me what Mike did to you?"

"Maybe one day," I said. "I dealt with it wrong, though."

"You don't say."

"You're the first person I've told about the *Inquirer* and probably the last. Dad and Mom found out and Officer Petersen figured it out."

"And how many months were you two at it?"

"Seven."

"Make much money?"

"Paid off our student loans and then some."

"Impressive."

"Thanks."

Alek was missing the northern lights and his gaze made my cheeks feel warm, but I didn't want him to stop looking at me that way.

"If I ever find myself in Vancouver, can I give you a call?" he asked.

"I would like that."

"In order to do that, you would need to trust me with your number."

"Give me your phone," I said.

But he kissed me instead.

CHAPTER 44

I WOKE TO THE SMELL OF BACON, EGGS, HASH BROWNS, AND TOAST wafting into my bedroom. A big breakfast for a big day. I hadn't meant to sleep in, but I hadn't meant to stay out until two a.m. either.

After breakfast with my parents, I got dressed in yoga pants and a t-shirt, pulled my hair into a ponytail, and didn't apply a bit of makeup because I just didn't feel like it. Almost everything was already packed. I stuffed my pajamas and bathroom kit into my biggest suitcase and zipped it up.

"You forgot these," Mom said from the doorway. She held up my bottle of anxiety pills.

"Flush them down the toilet," I said.

"It's not that easy and we both know it," she said. "Doesn't hurt to keep them handy."

She was right. It didn't take one day, a week, or even a summer to develop the anxiety problem and it would take longer to remedy, if ever. I put the pills in my backpack. I really did travel with a lot of baggage.

"Take this, too," Mom said. She pulled a cheque from the front pocket of her jeans. Payment for my work that summer. I didn't want to take the cheque, but Mom would have mailed it if I left it behind. I would need the money until I found another part-time job. I still hadn't told my parents about being fired from the bistro, but decided enough truths had been revealed for now. My monthly payments for my new student loan—through the bank of Dad the way the first should have been—started next month.

After my third and final trip hauling luggage to my Jeep, I sat on the porch with Mom and Dad. I was sad to say goodbye and yet excited for the next chapter. I wondered if that was how Dad felt while he watched the Hayeses load the herd, so I asked him.

"Something like that," he said with an amused snort.

We had already discussed everything that needed to be discussed and were waiting for Mike of all people. Even from outside, I thought I could hear Mom's clocks ticking. Mike had been due to arrive at eleven to pick up his July paycheque, and it was twenty minutes past. Maybe after last night's visit, he wasn't going to show up. I was leaving at noon regardless. At last his pickup truck lumbered up the driveway.

"I've changed my mind, Judith," Dad said. "Get my shot-gun. I should have shot him years ago when I had the chance." He smiled at me. Mom rolled her eyes, but her back was so straight that I thought she might get the shotgun.

Mike hopped out of his truck wearing a pair of jeans, a grey t-shirt, and a ball cap. If he was hungover, he didn't show it. Coca-Cola could have him.

"Good morning, everyone," he said as he climbed the porch steps.

"G'day," Dad said. He held up a cheque. Mike took it, folded it in half, and put it in his back pocket.

"I see you've got the wolf list out," Mike said. He was avoiding looking at Mom and me. Did he really think we hadn't told Dad about the night before, if nothing else? Did he think his behaviour was acceptable? Then I realized that he probably did. I had doubted myself and said little for years. People in general didn't like confrontation. Even if they were thinking someone was a jerk, they didn't usually say as much directly. It wasn't polite or productive. Maybe Mike was relying on that.

"You can thank Travis for us, but we won't be needing the extra hand around here anymore," Dad said.

Maybe some things do happen the way they do in the movies. Mike didn't seem to know what to say. Mom and Dad didn't stick around to let him think of something either. They went inside, leaving Mike and me on the porch alone. For the past week, I had imagined our final scene together, but after last night I realized that I had already said everything I had needed to say to Mike two years ago. He was the one who wanted to talk to me.

"Last night I came to see you, not your mother," he said in lieu of apologizing.

I sighed. Of course, I was at fault. It was a never-ending cycle. I didn't believe Mike wanted me back. I believed he felt entitled to the choice. He was miserable and wanted me to be miserable. Something had changed over the summer, but it wasn't Mike. I pitied him. He hadn't changed and probably never would.

"Are we going to talk about us?" he asked.

"There is no us. And I did nothing wrong legally, but I can't stop you if you want to raise a fuss about it," I said. The illusions I had had about him and about us were gone. I wasn't foolish enough to get too near him, and I watched my words with him, though. "I'm leaving, Mike. Take care of yourself."

After he left, I said goodbye to Mom and Dad. As I drove away, I glanced at the farm in the rear-view mirror and at the end of the drive stopped to take a long look at the Hayes farm down the road. This time I wasn't running away. I was moving on.

The Kingsley

Friday, September 25, 2015

GAZETTE

$2

kingsleygazette@freemail.com

NEW & IMPROVED

Former Gazette publisher Jack Whitby merges the best of Kingsley's two former newspapers

I wore the hats of writer, editor, and publisher for the *Kingsley Gazette* for seventeen years. It was a difficult but necessary decision to close the newspaper doors when my late wife Bette-Joan became ill in the summer of 2014.

I thank everyone for their thoughts, prayers, and helping hands in our hour of need. Bette-Joan was right on so many things, as she so often liked to remind me, but she was most right when she said we were blessed to live in a town like Kingsley.

Thank you to the *Inquirer* team for speaking to and for the community these past eight months. It is important for our small town to keep its voice lest we get lost in this big ol' world. The *Inquirer* was a controversial presence in our community, but I wish to acknowledge some of its positives and infuse them with our familiar old friend the *Gazette*

and its more traditional reporting style.

As you can see, we gave the *Gazette* a facelift. Yes, 'we.' This old man is working as part of a team to meet all of Kingsley's reporting needs. Each cover will announce points of interest and every issue will have regular columns, including Letters to the Editor, Sports & Entertainment, Lifestyle, Dear Deirdre, Classifieds & Announcements, and the Community Calendar.

I am proud to be back with the *Gazette* serving our community.
— Jack Whitby

CONTRIBUTIONS WELCOME!

Is there something Kingsley should know about? E-mail us or drop a note in our contributions box located at Kingsley Grocery. We want to hear from you.

ISSUE HIGHLIGHTS

CHAPTER 45

KIDS ARE HONEST. THEY WILL TELL YOU TO YOUR FACE IF YOU'RE FAT, have something in your teeth, or smell funny. Okay, sometimes too honest. But they are also quick to smile and to forgive. There is nothing better than seeing the joy on their faces when they understand something for the first time.

When I got back to Vancouver, I called about that tutoring job. The position I had applied for was filled, but a new one had opened up for September. My job was helping elementary kids with their homework after school while they waited for their parents to pick them up after work. Best of all, no newspapers!

Nathan still works for the *Gazette,* though his role is minimal compared to when we published the *Inquirer.* He also picks up the occasional shift at the Pink Rooster and is a full-time Journalism student at UBC. Joanna Petersen has taken over advertising and publication, while her dad and Nathan share the writing duties. Nathan's baby is the Lifestyles column. Occasionally Dad and Concerned Citizen get together to watch sports, during which nothing to do with the Inquirer is ever mentioned.

Nathan and I started playing what we call the *Inquirer* game. We talk to each other in headlines. The headlines are the only part of the *Inquirer* I miss, and coming up with them is a hard habit to break.

Bye-Bye Debt! Nathan sent Dad a cheque for forty-five hundred dollars. Only three more months sparing every dime I can from my tutoring job and I will have Nathan paid back for my share.

Miah Fights Back! Former *Inquirer* Lawyer Steps In Although in lawyer-speak you need *consensus ad idem*—a meeting of the minds—when signing a document, my student loan had been paid off and in Kingsley speak that means no harm, no foul.

Danika Texts Nathan ... But Still No Love for Former BFF! I am surprised I haven't heard much from Danika. Should I be surprised? I shouldn't be surprised.

Mike Replaced by Finley?! Dad took my advice and called Finley. Finley was jobless, knew how to run a combine, and wasn't my ex. Perfect.

Alek's Impending Visit Has Miah Over the Moon Best of all, Alek is flying to Vancouver for five days. Then we are driving back to Alberta together for the Thanksgiving long weekend.

How's Mike? Mike Who? My therapist says that the average abused woman tries seven times, whether she actually packs her suitcase or simply thinks she has made up her mind, before she successfully leaves her abuser. For a long time, I couldn't lump myself in with that group of women. Mike had never hit me, after all. If he had, I would have left. I think. I had left Mike for the seventh time this past summer, before I even left Kingsley.

Amiah, AJ, Miss Williams, Miah, Man-Eater, or Girl Next Door. No matter what people choose to call me, I am me. This is me; this is my side of the story. As Dad would say, take it or leave it.

RULES

1. Whatever is in the contributions box is published as long as ...   a) it has a grain of truth.
           b) it doesn't land us in court, jail, or early graves.

2. Stay neutral and anonymous.

3. Acknowledge there's always another side to every story.

4. Hook readers with the headline.

5. Keep articles short and snappy.

6. Don't let others do what you can do yourself (avoid third parties whenever possible).

7. Keep informants comfortable.

8. Keep advertisers happy.

9. When in doubt, ask a lawyer.

10. Quit while you're ahead.

11. Don't spend money you don't have.

ACKNOWLEDGEMENTS

DREAM MADE SWEETER BY DREAM TEAM

Thank you to NeWest Press, especially editor extraordinaire Leslie Vermeer, marketing guru Claire Kelly, and steadfast manager Matt Bowes. Also, to cover designer Kate Hargreaves who has perfectly reflected my vision for this controversial small-town paper.

LIES, SCANDAL, MURDER!

We went through a lot, my fiction workshopping group, supervisor Nicholas Royle, and I. The rigorous program through Manchester Metropolitan University resulted in not only my dissertation (aka *The Inquirer*), a master's degree, and an unforgettable graduation trip, but also a push to go public with my creative writing.

MENTOR'S THREAT EXPOSED

Looking to make a career out of my passion for words, I developed my professional writing and communication skills at MacEwan under the expert eyes of Leslie Vermeer and Lucille Mazo. Publishing Prose instructor Curtis Gillespie told me I wasn't meant to write just instruction manuals. His continued mentorship and confidence ensured I never forgot that.

LOTTERY WINNER!

I hit the jackpot with my ever-supportive and well-humoured parents Jim and Holly and brother Jesse. They've been reading my stories since the days they were written in crayon and listening to them even longer. My brother even knew we needed a librarian in the family, my sister-in-law Nikki, who I can always count on to read drafts.

JACLYN SAYS: 'I COULDN'T HAVE WRITTEN A BETTER PARTNER'

Thank you to my husband Logan. On top of everything else he does so well, he ensures that when I am too grounded, I get my head back in the clouds and write. He is the brave one who encourages me to be me and loves me for it.

MY GREATEST ADVENTURE!

I am forever grateful for my son, Seth. I've been reading and creating stories with and for him his entire life. My unofficial elementary-aged agent/publicist, he manages to work into a surprising number of conversations that his mom is now an author. Nonetheless, he can't possibly be as proud of me as I am of him.

IT TAKES A CRAZY VILLAGE

Thank you to my first readers and future readers, and to all those who believed in me along the way.

Jaclyn Dawn grew up in a tabloid-free small town in Alberta. With a communications degree and creative writing Masters, she works as a freelance writer and instructor. She now lives somewhere between city and country outside Edmonton with her husband and son. *The Inquirer* is her debut novel.